Out of this world... and into others

Out of this world... and into others

SHEELAGH MAWE

TOTALLY UNIQUE THOUGHTS

© 2008 TUT Enterprises, Inc.

Published by Totally Unique Thoughts®
　　　　A Division of TUT® Enterprises, Inc.
　　　　Orlando, Florida
　　　　http://www.tut.com

Printed in Canada on acid-free paper.

Cover Design by Andy Dooley.

Library of Congress Control Number: 2008909951

10 Digit ISBN 0-9642168-4-1
13 Digit ISBN 978-0-9642168-4-6

Dedicated to all those who wonder ...

Contents

Beth -
Here and there,
now and then ...

B eth Randall is not sleeping well. Her body twitches under the covers and occasional, incoherent sounds escape her lips.

Beside her in the king-size bed they share, her husband, Cliff, sleeps soundly, undisturbed by Beth's occasional kicks and nudges, her muttered grunts. Cliff learned a long time ago that someone as compulsively busy and preoccupied as Beth does not have a convenient OFF switch when sleep makes its demands.

It is nearly dawn and outside a beat-up jalopy turns into the Randall's street of pricey homes. From its depths, a paper boy starts flinging the day's news onto manicured lawns. As he approaches the Randall's two-storey Colonial, the automatic lawn-sprinkler heads come out of hiding and jets of water arc across the lawn.

Leering, taking careful aim, the kid at the wheel of the jalopy lets fly and whoops with joy as he achieves a bulls-eye on the central jet with a rolled up newspaper.

Inside the house a dog barks his indignation at this breach of silence, while upstairs an alarm clock, as though reminded of its daily chore, erupts into relentless beeping.

3

Beth reaches out and fumbles it into silence while Cliff puts a restraining hand on her shoulder.

"Tell me you're not getting up now," he groans. "It's still dark out there..."

By way of reply, Beth throws aside the bed covers and struggles to her feet beside the bed.

"But... it's too darned early," Cliff complains.

Sighing with exasperation, Beth heads for the bathroom. "Don't tell me you've forgotten," she hisses. "Jane graduates today, for heaven's sake!"

"Yeah, right... Not until eleven, though," Cliff calls after her. "That gives us a good couple more hours of sleep."

"How can you say that?" Beth squawks. "I've got to get in my run, you know that! And I have that eight-thirty appointment I told you about. I've still got a million calls to make..." she comes out of the bathroom dressed for running. "... The caterers. The other kids. Your folks. My folks. Got to remind everybody of everything else nothing will get done. Like always."

Cliff shakes his head, rolls his eyes, turns over and, clutching a pillow, goes back to sleep. Beth eyes his inert body with scorn, then turns and leaves the room, slamming the door behind her.

Downstairs in the kitchen, with frequent looks at the clock, Beth lets the dog out into the fenced backyard, pulls on her running shoes, makes a pot of coffee, does a few stretching exercises against the doorframe, then lets herself out the front door.

Almost at once she sees the sodden newspaper and, snarling with indignation, picks it up and tosses it on to the front porch. "That kid was mine..." she mutters.

Clicking on her stopwatch, she takes off running through the brightening day—a day that is spectacular in its clear, cool beauty if she'd allowed herself the luxury of taking it in. But Beth isn't like that. Beth's head teems, as always, with the myriad details that demand her strictest attention: her family, her clients, her home...

It's full day when she turns back into her driveway and now she is feeling good about herself. Her run went well. In fact, better than well. She knocked a quarter of a second off yesterday's time and, That's not bad for an old broad like me, she tells herself, getting out the blender and stuffing it with fruit, grains and a mix of vitamins. She holds the blender lid down with one hand while with the other she takes a couple of sweet rolls out of the freezer and, with a look of disgust, puts them in the microwave.

Again, both hands moving simultaneously, ably living up to the nickname "Windmill" given her by her children, Beth pours the contents of the blender into a glass, drinks it, turns on the TV, lets the dog in, feeds it and retrieves the sweet rolls from the beeping microwave.

"You up, Cliff?" she barks into the intercom. "Your

coffee's ready. Sweet rolls, too..."

She pauses, frowns, goes on in a gentler tone. "Please come down now, honey. There's such a lot to go over."

Cliff bounces into the kitchen, beaming, grabs Beth around the waist and swings her in a wide circle.

Exasperated, Beth detaches herself and glowers at her husband's attire.

"You can't go to your daughter's graduation ceremony dressed for golf!" she spits. "I laid out your suit, your tie, socks..."

"I'm just going to spend an hour on the practice range, OK? I'll be back in plenty of time to change."

Beth takes a deep breath not to scream, strives for a reasonable tone of voice. "But, honey! There's no way I'll have time to come back and get you. You'll have to shower, shave, dress. I told you last night I had an eight-thirty appointment."

"I know! I heard! It's not a problem. There's no need for you to come back. We'll go in separate cars, that's all."

Again, Beth fights to stay calm, "OK, OK," she mutters, "separate cars. But..." she pauses in the doorway of a room off the kitchen that is obviously an office, to glare at her husband, "DO NOT be late!"

Generally, Beth prides herself on keeping her office as neat and organized as the rest of her house and her life but this morning it is chaotic. Fabric and carpet samples are strewn everywhere and wallpaper books are piled precariously one on top of the other on the floor. Even her prized and beautifully framed diplomas—diplomas that proclaim her to be a fully licensed Interior Decorator—seem to hang askew.

Impatiently kicking aside copies of Architectural Digest, Beth strides to her desk, pushes aside family photographs showing her and Cliff with three, picture-perfect children at various stages of growth, and reaches for her Rolodex. Glancing at an antique wall clock, she punches numbers into the desk phone.

While she waits for the phone to be answered, her fingers drum the desktop but her stance and attitude change dramatically as the phone is picked up at the other end. In a voice scarcely recognizable from the one she so recently used on Cliff, she coos, "Mrs. James! Beth here. How are you? Just calling to confirm our eight-thirty appointment. I'll be there right on time with the samples you ordered. You're going to just love them..."

She pauses to listen, frowns, "You need another half hour? Nine o'clock, you say? But..." she looks at clock, rolls her eyes. "All right, Mrs. James, nine o'clock it is. Bye-eee."

She hangs up, muttering, "Lazy, bad-tempered old hag!" then punches in another number.

"Jimmy! Hi, honey. Hope you guys are up. Just calling to remind you and Betsy you need to leave by 9:45 to get to Jane's graduation on time. Jimmy..." Beth swivels to look at a blank TV screen, "I *know* I called last night but the TV says traffic is already heavy for this time of day and we simply can *not* be late. Oh, and remind Betsy to wear the pink, OK?" Beth listens, interrupts, "Yes, I do know she's an adult, honey, and I do know she's your wife but this is a once-in-a-lifetime, family event. There'll be photographs and..."

She frowns, shakes phone, hears dial tone, slams it down, "Kids!" she spits. "Can't tell 'em anything anymore."

Shaking her head, Beth pushes away from her desk, heads for the door, hesitates, goes back to phone, dials another number.

"Sarah! Sweetheart! Do me a favor will you and call your little brother, Jimmy, make sure he gets to the ceremony on time, OK? Now he's got caller ID I can't get through to him anymore. Oh... and honey... You will wear the blue, won't you? You look so gor... Sarah! Don't you dare hang up on me, too! Sa-rah!"

Livid, Beth slams the phone down and goes back to the kitchen.

"Cliff," she calls. "You still here?"

There is no answer from Cliff.

Seriously exasperated, Beth clears away his breakfast, dumps out coffee grounds, looks at the clock, yelps, runs for the stairs, takes them two at a time.

In the master bedroom, moving like a tornado, Beth hastily makes the bed, picks up Cliff's clothes and stuffs them into a hamper, lays his suit, shirt, tie, socks on the bed, places his shoes beneath them and heads for the shower peeling off her clothes as she moves.

Thirty-five minutes later, beautifully dressed, made up, and coiffed for the day ahead, Beth turns her SUV into the long driveway of an elegant mansion and parks to the side of the front door. Opening the rear doors of the van she pulls out fabric samples, wallpaper books, her briefcase, and staggers to the front door.

Burdened with her paraphernalia she sidles up to the doorbell and tries to ring it with her elbow. The books slip out of her hands and one lands on her foot. Wincing, hopping, biting back a curse, she fumbles with her now free hand and pulls a tissue out of her suit jacket pocket to dab at her sweating forehead and neck before taking another stab at the doorbell.

Chimes that would put Big Ben to shame peal out while Beth busies herself picking up her scattered samples. She is about to ring the doorbell again when the door creaks open and Hilda, the grim-faced housekeeper of the James residence, stands framed in the doorway.

"Hilda!" Beth exclaims. "How are you? You're looking chipper today! Would you please tell Mrs. James I'm here? She's expecting me."

"She didn't say nothing to me about it," Hilda says, her voice heavy with suspicion. "You sure?"

"Of course, I'm sure. I just spoke to her. She said nine o'clock."

"She's not down yet," Hilda says, stepping aside reluctantly to allow Beth entry.

Realizing honeyed tones are not going to cut it with Hilda, Beth changes tactics. "Just tell her I'm here, will you," she snaps, looking pointedly at her watch. "Today is a very busy day for me. My youngest daughter graduates from the University of Florida at eleven."

"It's not like it's her daughter, now is it?" Hilda sniffs. Turning, using the banister to pull herself along, she mounts the stairs at a snail's pace.

Biting back an angry retort, Beth sets down her samples, massages her aching forearms and paces the entry hall. She looks at her watch—9:05.

Ah! There are sounds coming from upstairs. Beth stops her pacing to listen. She hears a door opening. Muffled voices. Footsteps. Looking up she sees her client, Mrs. James, a sixty-ish matron, dressed in a robe and carrying a coffee mug, carefully descending the stairs.

"You're early, Beth," Mrs. James calls, sounding petulant. "I said 9:30."

"No!" Beth gasps. "We said nine. I wrote it down."

Realizing she is coming across as argumentative to her most prized client, Beth bites her lip, softens her approach.

"Um... Perhaps you're right. Maybe it was 9:30. Sorry. Can we begin?"

"Well, no... I have to freshen my coffee first," Mrs. James says peevishly. "You want some?"

"Why...uh... No thanks. What if I just arrange the samples in the living room while you get your coffee? You're going to just love them!"

Mrs. James grunts her assent and turns away to the kitchen while Beth totters into the living room with the samples. She props wallpaper samples against the walls, spreads fabric samples on various chairs, stands back to admire the effect, looks towards door expectantly.

Mrs. James is nowhere in sight. Beth scowls, looks at her watch, takes a deep breath, begins her ritual pacing, stops to rearrange her samples, paces some more.

Finally she goes to the door, puts a big smile on her face and calls out, "Yoo-hoo! I'm all ready for you, Mrs. James. Just wait till you see what I've brought you this time."

Mrs. James appears carrying a steaming mug of coffee. Beth beckons her forward with a flourish, "Ta-da!"

Mrs. James looks around the room slowly, her eyes taking in the various samples. She shakes her head.

"These are not at all what I had in mind, Beth" she growls. "Remember, I said I wanted a tropical look. Lots of green. Big, leafy prints. This..." her mouth turns down, "this stuff looks like Grandma Moses' attic. What were you thinking about?"

Beth takes a deep breath, ready to explode, then reminds herself that the customer is always right. Reaching for her briefcase, she pulls out her order book, flips pages, smiles winningly.

"You're just not used to seeing these prints in here," she reassures. "Look here," she flourishes her order book, "these are exactly what we ordered. Maybe it's just that they look smaller...? Bigger? Than they did in the book?"

"They don't look anything like what was in the book, Beth. These are... They're just plain awful! Good thing my husband's not here to see them. He'd fire you on the spot! We'll have to start over, that's all. Or..." she purses her lips, looks at Beth sideways, "maybe I should just start over with someone else?"

Beth bites her lower lip trying to remember why she'd been so eager to decorate for Mrs. James in the first place. Old bitch was known all over town as a decorator's nightmare.

Because I knew I could turn this frumpy old barn of a house into a dream home, she reminds herself. And by golly, I will! Just not today.

"Tell you what," she coos to Mrs. James. "Why don't I just leave these samples here over the weekend? You might find they grow on you. If not, why... I'll just come pick them up Monday and we'll start over."

"No, no, no! I want them out of here! NOW! Mr. James would take away my credit cards if he thought I was even considering this... This stuff. Besides, I won't be here Monday. I'll be out of town all next week. Let's have a look at whatever else you've got there now."

"Now? Beth fumbles. "But..."

"Yes, now! This is the second time you've done this to me, Beth. Ordered the wrong samples. Now, let's take a look at your other books and settle this once and for all. I expect to entertain in this room within the month."

Beth starts to jabber, then pulls herself up short. She knows she ordered exactly what Mrs. James requested and she won't be browbeaten.

Eyeing the woman square in the face, she says, "Mrs. James, I'm sorry you're not happy with *your* choices but I don't have time to show you any other samples today. I have to be on my way. My daughter graduates from the University of Florida," she looks at her watch, "in a little over one hour from now and I intend to be there. On time!"

"In Gainesville?" Mrs. James gasps. "You'll never make it. It's five to ten right now."

"That's because you didn't honor either your eight-thirty or nine o'clock appointment time," Beth snaps. "Now, if you'll just lend me Hilda for a few minutes we'll get these samples out of here and I'll be on my way."

Mrs. James' eyes widen with horror. "Hilda can't carry those great big heavy books of yours. Good Lord, she's in her sixties! They're way too heavy."

"I guess I'll just have to manage on my own then, won't I?" Beth says, barely able to restrain a sneer. "After all, I did bring them all in, didn't I?"

Mrs. James says nothing, merely leads the way to the

foyer and watches Beth struggle her samples to her car where she tosses them in amongst several, beautifully wrapped, graduation gifts.

Without a backward glance, Beth gets behind the wheel and drives away, gravel spitting from her rear tires. Slowing at the end of the driveway, she takes a quick look in the rearview mirror and sees both Mrs. James and Hilda watching her from the front steps.

"Old hags!" she says out loud. "Go ahead and rot in that hideous house! It's what you deserve."

Deep down, though, she knows she only has herself to blame. It was she who forced the morning's appointment when she could have waited till Monday and driven up to Gainesville with Cliff. But how was she supposed to know Mrs. James would be so inconsiderate? So rude?

Because, she tells herself, while fuming at a red light, everyone told you the old bat would be a nightmare to work with. But no, you wouldn't listen. Had to prove yourself right... Get your picture in the paper as "Our town's leading decorator," and now you've blown the whole deal.

Too late now, she shrugs. Besides, who was to say Cliff wasn't still at the club when, as a dutiful parent, he should be on his way to Gainesville right this minute.

Thinking that, she steps on the gas, swings on to the interstate and, though speed limit signs of 55 mph are posted at intervals along the highway, weaves in and out of traffic, one eye on her watch, the other on the speedometer until she is cruising at 70 mph.

"I'm coming, Jane, honey!" she calls, imagining her voice carrying across the miles. "I'm nearly there. You can count on me. I wouldn't be late for your graduation for the world. Trust me, OK?"

After what seems eternity, Beth sees signs on the Interstate reading, Gainesville Next Three Exits. She takes the second one, brakes for a red light at the bottom of the exit ramp, accelerates, then is forced to a crawl as she wends her way through heavy traffic and teeming pedestrians all heading for the University. She fumes at red lights, screams out loud as, time after time, she is unable to cross an intersection before the light reverts to red.

At the second-to-last major intersection she must cross prior to parking and, inching forward imperceptibly, she is nevertheless forced to sit through two complete changes. Then, even though the light has once again just turned to red, she grits her teeth and accelerates to get through anyway.

From the corner of her eye, she sees, too late, a car speeding towards her from the opposite direction. There is the howling shriek of both cars braking violently, then the sickening, heart-stopping thud of a head-on collision.

Headlights, hub caps, broken glass and bumpers litter the intersection. Both cars are destroyed. Pedestrians cluster, looking on in horror. Car horns from angry drivers too far back to be aware of the accident fill the air to be quickly drowned out by the urgent wailing of sirens as police cars and rescue vehicles approach from all directions.

While pedestrians scatter, some of the emergency vehicles mount the sidewalk to get through the heavy traffic and to the scene of the crash. Road blocks are quickly set up and police divert traffic.

* * *

It is 10:58 and a mile away, in the auditorium of the University of Florida, Beth's family anxiously studies every face entering through the multiple doorways. There is an empty seat in their midst. Beth's.

Abruptly, the graduation ceremony begins as capped and gowned students, accompanied by boisterous cheers from their beaming families, enter the auditorium from all four corners and file into the seats reserved for them.

At the accident scene, police cars are miraculously shunted aside to make room for ambulances. Broken, bloodied bodies are extracted from the wreckage, placed on stretchers by paramedics and carried inside the vehicles where IVs are rapidly inserted. Then, sirens howling, the ambulances race away to nearby hospitals.

In the auditorium, numerous, tedious speeches come to an end and the graduates, upon hearing their names, mount the steps of the platform to be awarded their diplomas together with a handshake from the Governor.

When Jane Randall's name is called, her family cheers wildly even though they are confused and worried by Beth's absence.

The ceremony over, the students crowd outside to meet with their families where they are hugged, kidded, congratulated and photographed.

The Randall family is no exception except their euphoria is severely dampened by Beth's absence and their conversation verges on the hysterical as each member tries to reassure the others.

"Take a look at the traffic!"

"Way worse than other years…"

"She'll just be heartsick to have missed seeing you graduate, Jane, honey!"

"But hey, no sweat! We got it all on tape!"

"She'll see just what we saw. Every precious second…"

"Come on, let's eat. Bet she couldn't get through the traffic and is waiting for us at the restaurant."

"How will she know which restaurant we'll be at?" Jane asks.

"Who do you think made the reservation?" answer her siblings in unison.

Jane and Sarah get in their father's car while Jimmy and his wife, Betsy, follow in their own. After wending their way out of the parking lot, the occupants of both cars are astonished by the heavy, scarcely moving traffic.

"No wonder your Mom didn't make it to the ceremony," Cliff says to Jane. "This is the worst jam I've seen in years. Was yours a bigger than usual graduating class?"

Jane shrugs. "If it was, nobody told me about it. Do you think Mom might still be stuck in all this somewhere?"

"I doubt that," Cliff says. "You know what a stickler for punctuality she is. Bet she was in town on time but seeing the situation, and knowing she'd be late for the ceremony—she wouldn't have wanted to draw attention to herself by coming in late—I bet she went straight to the restaurant like we said earlier. Now it's her turn to wait for us. You are still trying to get her on her cell phone, right?"

Betsy and Sarah both nod, try Beth's number again and, receiving no answer, looking disgusted, settle in for a long, tedious wait.

Stalled at an intersection where a policeman is directing traffic, Cliff lowers his window and calls out to a bystander. "You have any idea what the hold-up is?"

"Accident down the road a ways," comes the reply. "Some kid ran a red light from what I hear. Both cars totaled. Injuries..."

"Thanks," Cliff says, closing his window. He turns to the girls, "You heard him same as me. Some kid ran a red light. And there you have it. Chaos for the rest of the world."

"Poor Mom," Betsy sighs. "Hope she at least made it to the restaurant."

* * *

At the intersection where the accident took place, tow-trucks have hauled away the damaged vehicles. Broken glass and auto parts have been swept away and traffic, both pedestrian and otherwise, crowd the streets and sidewalks as before.

Beth is standing at the northwest corner of the intersection. She looks confused and repeatedly rubs her forehead. She looks at her watch and sees that it has stopped.

Exasperated, she approaches a group of pedestrians who are waiting for the light to change. "Excuse me. My watch seems to have stopped," she says, forcing a smile. "Can any of you tell me what time it is?"

The talking, laughing group ignores her and she looks after them in dismay as they step into the crosswalk and traverse the street.

Ah! She spies half-a-dozen elderly people coming her way. Certain of a courteous response from such a kindly-looking group, she again asks for the correct time. Again she is ignored. Baffled, she looks after them, wondering what is wrong with people nowadays. Or is it her? Is there a smudge on her face? Her lipstick crooked? Her hair a mess? What?

Maybe I look like I feel, she thinks ruefully. Kind of out of it... Head buzzing and popping as if I've just come through a tunnel... That, or as though I'm on a plane that's begun its descent. If I could get rid of it, she thinks, rubbing her forehead again with the heel of her palm, I could maybe put on a happier face, get someone to talk to me.

And this awful thirst! Where did that come from? She gropes for her bottle of imported water, always kept tucked in an outer pocket of her purse, then comes to a shocked standstill realizing she's not carrying her purse. She fights not to panic. Where is it? She must have left it somewhere. But... where? Her money is in it! Her credit cards! All her ID!

Aghast, she wonders just what in hell is going on. Like for starters, where is she? She doesn't recognize a thing. Can't seem to remember where she is—was—going.

Obviously, what she needs to do first is find a water fountain. Then a place to sit for a minute, catch her breath, get herself together and then... Then she'll be able to figure it all out. She continues along the sidewalk certain of only one thing: she is late for something although she cannot, for the life of her, think what it is.

Up ahead she sees a park bench in the shade of a large and beautiful oak and quickens her pace. Exactly what she needs. Seating herself with a sigh of relief, she closes her eyes, takes a few deep, practiced breaths, works at calming, centering, herself.

That's better, she reassures herself. Much better. Doing good now. Staying calm. Staying cool. Any minute now you're going to know—remember—everything. Where you are. Where you left your purse. Your next appointment. Just take it easy a little while longer and you'll be fine. Keep on breathing deep now. Just a few more and you can open your eyes, get a bearing on where you are, take it from there.

Slowly, Beth allows her eyelids to open. OK, she's facing a parking lot. She scans the parked cars wondering if hers is among them. Nope, doesn't seem to be. But... no panicking, she reminds herself sharply. If it's not here then it's somewhere nearby, else how did you get here in the first place?

On the other side of the lot she sees a group of people turn in off the sidewalk. They chat briefly then get into two cars parked side by side. With a jolt of dismay she realizes she is staring at her own family.

Memory returns with a blinding flash. Jane's graduation! Of course! That's where she was going. They all were. But then... How come she's here and they're over there? And what are any of them doing in this parking lot? Won't they be late for the ceremony? But look! Jane is with them. Does that mean...? Could it mean that she somehow missed the ceremony? She couldn't have! It would be unthinkable! Impossible! She'd never miss the graduation of her baby. But then... why isn't she with them? And how did she get here?

Even while her brain thus churns she is on her feet running, calling their names, dodging in and out of parked cars, calling louder, running faster, panting, sobbing...

She sees the doors of the two cars slam shut, brake lights momentarily light up, then one after the other, the cars back out and, with loud shouts of, "See you in a minute," and waving arms, follow each other out of the lot.

Though her instinct is to keep running, calling, Beth slumps despairingly against the nearest car knowing they hadn't seen her, couldn't have heard her. She also knows, remembers, that she has no car herself. No purse, no money, no credit cards, no phone, no ID.

A bitter sob of frustration escapes her followed by an even louder snort of derision, for in running towards her family, she had noticed that neither Sarah nor Betsy had worn the pink and blue dresses she had recommended.

So much for your priorities, darling, she tells herself with a sneer. And now what? Although panic is still an issue, threatens, in fact, to suffocate her, one of Beth's highest priorities has always been to stay in control and she fights to maintain it now.

Listen, she reasons with herself, at least now you know where you are. You're in Gainesville, OK? Your family is here, too. That puts you way ahead of where you were a couple of minutes ago. Now go back to that bench and figure where you go from here. Seems like a police station would be your best bet. Cliff—all of them—have got to be worrying, wondering where you are. Maybe they've reported your absence?

She cringes inwardly, stifles a sob, realizing that if she went to the police she'd be turning herself in as a missing person. But she's not missing, is she? She's right here where she's supposed to be.

Still making her way back towards the bench, still desperate for water, Beth becomes aware of a young kid on a skateboard—thirteen, fourteen maybe, baggy shorts, faded T-shirt, baseball cap on backwards—who she realizes has been circling her like a gnat for some time. She wants to tell him to buzz off, but then she brightens. Maybe he can at least give her the correct time, direct her to a nearby water fountain, and then, well... who knew?

The kid does a wide loop around her, stops with a flourish to face her, upending his skateboard with his foot and catching it with one hand even as he grins and says, "Hey, Beth. Sorry I'm late!"

Taken aback, Beth gasps, "Do I know you?"

"Kind of..."

"Well... I... um... What's your name?"

"Ben."

"Oh. Nice name. I used to know... That is, I once had... Anyway, what do you mean, you're late? Late for what?"

"I was supposed to meet you."

"Meet me? Here? In the middle of a street I don't even know the name of?"

"Yep. This is the place all right only like I said, I got held up... Kind of... I'm late."

"I don't know what you're late for but I know I am.... I was on my way..." Beth falters, "to my youngest daughter's graduation ceremony."

She looks around, frowns. "Only... I seem to have lost my way somehow. Lost my watch, too.'

Ben nods sympathetically.

"Well, do you at least know what time it is? We were supposed to have a celebration lunch after the ceremony. Maybe I can catch up with them at the restaurant, *The Beehive*, find out what's going on."

Ben holds up both wrists showing he is not wearing a watch. "Doesn't matter what time it is anymore," he says with a grin. "You've got all the time in the world now, Beth."

"I do not! What a ridiculous thing to say. I need to catch up with my family before they leave the restaurant... If that's where they went. I must catch up with them. I need them to help me find my car." She falters, shakes her head. "This is all just so weird. How could I lose my car?"

Ben shrugs. "Happens to everybody once in a while. No big deal."

Beth snorts, "Maybe not to some, but to me it's a very big deal."

"Come on," Ben says, "It's just a car. You can..."

"Just a car," Beth repeats, scorn in her voice. "You don't

know what you're saying. Every important document I own just happens to be in it. I've got to..." she pauses, a look of wonder on her face. "You know something? I think I just figured out what's happening to me. I'm dreaming!" she looks around the street, the parking lot, waves her arms to take it all in. "When I wake up I'll laugh about all this... This confusion."

"I guess you could think that," Ben says slowly. "Only, believe me, you're not. Dreaming, I mean. This is for real. Come on, I'll take you home. We can talk more about it there."

In spite of herself, Beth bursts out laughing. "You're going to take me home? On a skateboard?"

"You don't need wheels to get where you're going now, Beth. All you have to do is think, 'Home' and you're there."

"OK. OK. Whatever you say. People always say weird things in dreams, don't they? But listen, since you seem to want to be helpful—even if you are a figment of my imagination—why don't you tell me where *The Beehive* restaurant is. Maybe walk me there so I can check it out. That's where I made the reservation." She pauses, rubs her forehead. "Wait a minute, if I'm dreaming why would I do that? All I have to do is wake up in my own bed..."

"Right. That's where you need to be now, Beth," Ben agrees. "Home. In bed if you want. Come on I'll take you. Just think about it and you'll be there."

"Why would I?" Beth asks. "Since I'm already home. Now I can wake up. Make some calls..." she pauses, frowns, puts her hands to her ears to drown out a loud swooshing sound. At the same instant she realizes that she and Ben are standing in the entry hall of a magnificent home.

"This isn't my home," she splutters. "I only wish! This is more like my dream home." She walks slowly around the ground floor, nodding with approval at everything she sees, stopping here and there to touch and marvel at various beautiful items. She pauses to look upwards. "Wow! Whoever did the lighting in here is a genius," she exclaims. "Not a lamp or a light bulb or even a candle in sight and yet such clarity, such warmth. Almost golden, wouldn't you say? Wonder how they did it?"

She pauses again to sniff appreciatively, "And the smell! Are you getting it? Wonderful, isn't it? Like... Like every flower you ever heard of but more, too. You know, roses. A touch of jasmine. Gardenias. Lilacs..."

Ben nods. "Yeah! Great smells. But, hey! Let me tell you where we are. This is the home that, room by room, you dreamed about your whole life. Everything in here is something you at some time admired. Longed for."

"You're right!" Beth exclaims. "That's why it all looks so familiar. But... How did it get here?"

"It got here because, like I said, you thought about it. Imagined having it."

"But I wanted it in my house!" Beth wails in

exasperation. "Not here!"

"Why not here? This is your house. The one you always imagined living in but never allowed yourself to have. The one you thought you couldn't afford. So... You got what you thought about."

Beth shakes her head in confusion. "I have no idea what you're talking about," she says. "And frankly I'm having too much fun to care. This is some dream. Maybe I'll take my time waking up after all. Show me some more!"

Ben leads her into a cozy den where a fire burns brightly in the hearth. "Have a seat," he says, "put your feet up. Relax. I'll go get you a cup of tea. Earl Gray, isn't it?"

"How can you possibly know I like Earl Gray tea?"

Ben shrugs, laughs, "Why wouldn't I? Anyway, there's no other brand in the pantry, I checked. Be right back."

Beth leans back in a luxurious leather recliner, puts her feet up, sighs with pleasure as soft music begins to play. She notices the shelves facing her are crowded with photographs and she leans forward a little to study them, a bemused expression on her face. They look familiar, but... she settles back, too comfortable to get up and examine them more closely.

She's interrupted by the return of Ben with drinks, tea with lemon for her, Coke for him.

"Nice touch, the lemon," Beth smiles, raising her cup

towards him as though in a toast, then taking a sip. "Tastes just like the real thing, too. Imagine that! Tea that tastes like tea in the middle of a dream."

Leaning back she takes the time to study Ben carefully. "Don't I know you from somewhere?" she asks. "You look like... You look a bit like my Jimmy. Same kind of lanky build. He's my eldest son, you know. Then again, there's something of Sarah around your eyes, your nose..."

Ben shrugs, "Could be."

"And your name is Ben?" Beth sets aside her cup and saucer, shakes her head. "This is weird. You have no idea how very weird. You know what, though? While this is all very nice," she waves her hand taking in their surroundings, "when I said I wanted to go home, I didn't mean to a dream home, gorgeous as this all is. I meant I wanted to go to my real home. The one I live in every day with my family. In that home any minute now the old alarm clock is going to ring and I'll be heading out the door to run my five miles..." she pauses, rubs her forehead, "I'm going to wake up now, Ben. But before I do I'd like you to know that this is about the strangest dream I've ever had. I mean, it started out as such a nightmare and then you came along and it's been kind of fun. Weird, but fun. I don't know if you can but is there any way you can explain how come..."

"Tell you what," Ben interrupts hastily, "There's this new DVD that just came in. Why don't you just take a couple more minutes to watch it? It's really cool. Then we can talk."

Beth settles back with a groan. "Sure. What's another couple minutes. Beats running five miles."

Ben turns on DVD.

Beth sees a baby being christened. "I baptize you Elizabeth Veronica Lauderhill," intones the priest, making the sign of the cross on the infant's forehead with his thumb.

Beth's eyes bug. "That's my name!" she yelps. "Was... Before I married Cliff, I mean."

Ben nods in agreement.

The tape goes on to show a rapidly moving montage of a life. Beth toddling, going to kindergarten, jumping rope, sassing her parents. Attending Girls scouts. Taking riding lessons. Beth smiling sweetly. Beth howling with rage. There are a few close-ups of Beth being kind, many of her being cruel and unkind. Then comes her marriage and the birth of her own children. Scenes of Beth mothering, sometimes beaming, sometimes scowling. Beth sobbing in despair beside the coffin of an infant.

Even as she sobs in the movie, Beth sobs watching it. "That was my baby." she explains, her voice muffled by her hands. "My precious Ben. He only lived for a few days. I've never gotten over it."

Ben hands her tissues, nods as though understanding.

The DVD continues through many more phases of

Beth's life up to where she is talking to her daughter, Jane, on the phone.

"I'm just so thrilled about your upcoming graduation, honey," she chirps, beaming. "This will be a dream come true for your father and me. All our wonderful kids 'launched' at last. What a day it will be to see you going up to get your diploma. I can't wait!"

Beth sees clips of her early morning run, talking to Cliff, her meeting with Mrs. James. Then she's on the highway, in traffic, screaming at red lights. Next come scenes and sounds of a hideous traffic accident and the screen goes blank.

Beth comes upright, horrified. "What was that?" she gasps. "How did that get in there? What..."

"That was your life, Beth." Ben says quietly.

"Was? It is my life. All except that last part, I mean. That wreck or whatever it was. I've never been in a wreck. Believe me, if I had, particularly one like that, I'd remember it. I remember everything else though. Just like in the movie I got up this morning to drive up to Jane's graduation. I had to really push the pedal to get to Gainesville on time and then... I don't know... Seems like I've been in a fog ever since. Still don't know where I parked. Don't know where I left my purse. How come that wasn't on the screen? And how about you showing up and bringing me to..." she shrugs, blinks, looks around, "wherever this is?

"I don't understand any of it. I don't like it! It's gone

on way too long. I mean, where did that movie come from, anyway? Who made it? You're scaring me half to death, you know. I need to wake up now, Ben. Now!"

"You are awake, Beth," Ben insists quietly. "More awake than you've ever been. All that other? Those scenes of your life? That was the dream. Just a blink in eternity. This is where you came from. This is where you return. You're home now, Beth. Really home."

"I am not! I'm here!"

"Right. And you're here because you left the earth in that accident, Beth. You died. At least that's how you earth-ies think of it. Over here we know there is no such thing as death; that we all live throughout eternity. You're here now for a time-out, so to speak. A rest. And then, when you're up for it, you can go back to live a whole 'nother life."

Beth studies Ben carefully, opens her mouth to speak several times, says nothing. Her face shows astonishment, fear, disbelief. Finally, scorn.

"Dead?" she bursts out laughing. "Dead? I'd been in that accident, I'd have been smashed to pieces. Look at me. You see any broken bones, torn flesh, blood? 'Course not. Whatever else I am, take it from me, I'm not dead. I may have missed a beat somewhere in there. Missed out on Jane's graduation—I still haven't figured that one out—but I will.

"And now I'm going to wake up. I have to. I've got a lot going on right now. My darling Jane to welcome home, congratulate. Mrs. James' living room to finish up. Other deals in the making! Betsy and Jimmy's baby due in a couple months. The baby shower to organize..."

Ben rubs his hands over his face, mutters, "This isn't going like I planned." He turns to face Beth. "Look at it this way. Think of earth as a stage like... like Shakespeare said. And all the people there are actors playing their roles. Well, when the role is over what are they supposed to do, huh? Hang around forever? Go on hiatus? 'Course not. When the role's over, it's over. They leave, come back here. Your role there was over, Beth. Your time was up. You came home."

Beth is watching him with angry disbelief. "Don't be so ridiculous!" she spits. "Actors? A stage? My eye! Life is for real, Ben! People are born. They lead useful lives, make a contribution, take care of one another, have families and when the time comes, they die! Their bodies get buried. In catechism we were taught that a part of us called the "soul" goes to see God in heaven. He forgives us our sins and the angels sing and play harps.

"That's what happens when you die. Everybody knows that! You don't walk around a town with a strange kid on a skateboard. Visit "dream homes." Drink tea. Watch movies. If you only knew the funerals I've attended. My parents. Friends. Even my own child. My poor little baby, Ben..."

She stops in mid-sentence, stares in confusion at Ben.

"That's what it is about you! You remind me of him somehow. Even your name..." she gasps helplessly, "But he died! I know he did. You saw his funeral yourself in that movie."

Ben leans forward, clasps both Beth's hands. "I am that son, Beth. That's why they sent me to meet you. They figured..."

Beth's mouth drops open. Her eyes never leaving Ben, she pulls her hands free of his, gets unsteadily to her feet, steps backwards. "You're lying!" she hisses. "And you're crazy. My Ben was just days old when he died. He was a baby. You're big! Dead babies don't keep growing. They can't. And they don't dress like a punk. Chase around on a skateboard. Get in people's dreams. Just... Just go away!'

Ben looks around helplessly. "I guess I'm not doing too good, huh? You're my first death, see. They said you might take a lot of convincing but we thought for sure between me meeting you and your life review you'd get it. I mean, you *saw* the accident." He raises his voice in the direction of a half open door. "I need some help in here," he calls.

Beth hears the murmur of voices outside the door, stares dumbfounded as her parents enter the room. Not old or ill as she remembered them, but in the prime of life.

"What was in that tea you just gave me?" she gasps to Ben.

33

Ben stands up and addresses grandparents. "Guess I really screwed up, huh? Sorry."

Grandparents hug him, laugh with him. "You did just fine, kid," his grandfather beams. "First one's always tough. Especially when an accident's involved. It's the suddenness of it, see. The shock. Takes them longer to come to terms with it than others. You'll get the hang of it."

Both parents turn to Beth, arms outstretched, "Good to see you again, honey. Welcome home."

Beth clutches the back of the chair to steady herself. "I need to wake up!" she babbles. "Get out of here. This is crazy."

She turns to face her parents "Mom... Dad... I mean, good to see you and all but... I'm sorry, I just don't get this. I thought I was dreaming but... Well, now I don't know anything anymore. I don't understand what's going on. I met this kid in a parking lot. He tells me I'm dead, brings me here. Wherever here is. And now you come walking in. How did you get here? I thought... I mean, I *know* you... um... died a long time ago. I went to your funerals. But hey, you both look really great. I mean, you know, alive!"

"We are, honey! We are. Nobody dies. It was just time for us to move on to the next level. And that's what you just did. You moved on."

Beth turns away from all three, muttering. "Great! Here I am with three people I *know* are dead—even

34

though they all look very much alive to me. And they're trying to tell me *I'm* dead! I need to get away from them. But... how? If I'm not dreaming, I can't wake up, can I? So where do I go from here?"

Deeply confused by the whole situation, despairing of ever understanding any of it, Beth totters backwards into the recliner and bursts into heart-rending sobs.

Her mother hurries forward, kneels beside her and puts her arms around her. "Honey," she soothes, "It's OK. Really, I know just how you feel. We all do to some degree or another when we first get here. And it's always harder on those who have a violent death like you did in that nasty old wreck of yours. That's why we sent Ben to meet you. We thought for sure you'd recognize him. He's the very image of Cliff, don't you think? But we came, too, just in case. All of us here to help you adjust.

"What you need now is a good rest to clear your head and then you'll see how exciting and wonderful everything really is here. Just think, honey, you graduated!"

With a mighty effort at control, Beth stops crying, looks at her mother. "Mom," she begins, "I don't know where we are right now. In fact, I'm not sure of anything. But since you and Dad and Ben are so sure I'm ... I don't even want to say the word. Let's just say, if it's true I'm what you say I am, then prove it. Tell me. Better yet, show me. Where is God?"

"Where is God?" her mother gasps. "Why honey,

he's the same place he was... is... on earth. He's everywhere!"

"Everywhere," Beth repeats, looking around her blankly. "Sorry, Mom, but darned if I can see him. Don't see any angels with harps either. What happened to them and all the other things Sister Veronica at the Sacred Heart told us about?"

Her mother leans forward, "I'm remembering now how it was when I first got here," she confides. "I expected those kinds of things, too, but then I learned— was taught—that God isn't the bearded old man our religions tell us about. Instead, God is everything. Everywhere. Like I just said, there is a God spark in every living thing—every human, every animal, every plant. Without that spark, why they... you... me... wouldn't exist. God is All and He's everywhere."

"OK, Mom, OK. We can get back to him later. In fact, I'm sorry I asked. What I really need to get through to you right now though is that I AM NOT DEAD!

"I can't be. It wouldn't be fair. See, I'm only forty-six years old. Now it was probably different for you and Dad when you came... um... wherever we are. You were old. You'd both been sick a long time so when whoever-it-was told you you were dead, you just went along with them because... Well, because what else were you supposed to make of this beautiful place?

"But me, I still have a long way to go. I have responsibilities. Lots of them. There's Jane who just graduated. She needs me to help her find a job, get her set up in a place of her own. Jimmy and Betsy are expecting their first baby. I need to help them through that. Remember how you helped me? And then there's Cliff. You know how he depends on me. The man can't get himself dressed in the mornings if I don't lay out his clothes for him. I mean, I don't know how to get through to you but, whatever else I am, I'm NOT dead!"

"You're right, honey, you're right," her mother soothes, stroking Beth's hair. "You know why? Because there's no such thing. You're just in a different place, that's all. Let's go talk to your Dad. He's just always so proud of how well you and Cliff brought up those kids of yours. And, of course, we've both just had the best time with young Ben since he got here. He's the most wonderful young man. Everybody here loves him."

Rolling her eyes in exasperation, Beth follows her mother to the family room where her father and Ben are chatting in front of a TV. Her father hurries forward to embrace Beth once again.

"Damn, but it's good to see you," he says. "We've been counting the days, you know. And here you are, right on time!"

"Right on time?" Beth exclaims.

"Sure," her father says. "Right year, right day, right everything, down to the last second."

"But..." Beth stammers, "Who said? What are you talking about? You sound as though I made some kind of

37

appointment and I know I didn't. My next appointment was Jane's graduation and I... I missed it somehow." Tears well up in her eyes and she hangs her head.

Her father puts his arm around her shoulder just as her mother had done, and gives her a squeeze. "The time I'm talking about now is the time you decided on when you set out on your Beth adventure. See, back then you weren't long back from a life where you'd chosen to live into your nineties. And you did. Outlived your own kids while you were at it, too! Only thing was, you were bed-ridden the last fifteen years and in a lot of pain and discomfort as well. Couldn't do a thing for yourself in the end."

"A life where I chose to live into my nineties?" Beth gasps. "Me? You're not making sense. What do you mean?"

"We can talk about that life later," her father says. "Grumpy old soul you were at the end. Anyway, right then's when you said no more of that! Said, if ever I decide to go back, next time around I'll halve it. Check out at forty-six. Your Mom and I—Ben too—met you in what you'd call, "the dream state," and we agreed knowing we'd be back here ourselves by then. Only thing was," he nods towards Ben who is once again cruising around on his skateboard on the patio, "Mr. You-Know-Who there got a bit too caught up with that new toy of his and was a tad bit late meeting you."

"That's what he said when I met him," Beth says in

wonderment. "Said, 'Hi, Beth, sorry I'm late.'"

Her father and mother nod their heads in agreement. "There you have it," her father chuckles, somewhat ruefully, "But, what're you going to do, huh? Kids will be kids no matter where they are."

"Not my kids," Beth says with a toss of her head. "If I taught them anything it was to be punctual. Which is why I don't understand how I could have missed my beautiful Jane's graduation."

"Yeah, well... You're forgetting Ben wasn't with you long enough to get the punctuality message, now was he? Anyway, we can go over all that after you've had time to rest and get acclimatized," her Dad reassures her.

"Come on, Dad," Beth glowers, "No more talk about resting and dying and blah, blah, blah. If ever I could count on straight answers from anyone, it was from you and I need some now."

Looking sideways at her mother and Ben, she lowers her voice, "Can we go off somewhere quiet, just the two of us? Maybe out by the pool? And you can tell me," she stamps her foot, raises her voice, "just exactly what the hell is going on!"

"Sure, honey, sure," her dad agrees, "Come on, we'll do just that, go out by the pool. There's someone out there you need to meet, anyway. He's the one you really need to talk to."

"Dad," Beth interrupts, coming to a standstill. "I don't

want to meet—or talk—to anybody right now, OK? I'm not here to socialize, although," she hesitates, "I have no clue why I am here. All I want to do right now is talk to you. Can we do that or am I going to have to...?"

The two emerge on the pool deck and Beth is relieved to see no one else there. "I thought you said there was someone out here?" she says.

"Oh, he can take a hint," her father says. "He'll catch up with us later."

"Not if I can help it," Beth mutters. "Soon as you clarify a thing or two for me, I'm out of here. I've wasted enough time already."

Her father chuckles, "You've got all the time in the world now, sugar."

"That's another thing Ben said earlier," Beth scowls. "So let's start right there. What is that supposed to mean, 'All the time in the world'? And who the heck is he, anyway? Ben, I mean?"

"Let's take the second question first," her father suggests. "Ben *is* your son, honey. The one you lost in infancy."

Beth opens her mouth to protest but her father silences her by holding up his hand and shaking his head. "Let me finish," he says. "Listen to what I have to say and then we can go from there. As I said, Ben is your son. Before his birth to you—that is, when he was still here on this side—the three of you, Ben, Cliff and you had a get together in the dream state. You all agreed that he would only show up for a very short earth life with you this time around because what you all had to learn, while of extreme importance, could be taught quickly. And because he already had other commitments..."

Again he holds up his hand to silence Beth who is trembling with her need to speak. "You all made that choice because throughout the many lives you three shared over the centuries, none of you felt you had truly understood either the magnificence or the depths of life, nor fully experienced emotion. Most particularly, the emotion that comes with love. You have to realize that going way back in time, life—any life—was not seen as the miracle it is today. Disease was rampant. A simple cut or scrape could be fatal. Hygiene was unknown. Hunger prevalent. Wild animals stalked the night. People died decades earlier than they do now. Few babies survived their gestation period and many of those who did were lost in infancy. Expectations were low, then. Life was so hard, survival so paramount that few, if any, gave a thought beyond the morrow. It was eat or be eaten. Kill or be killed. Consequently, love as we now know it was an unknown in that experience. It was to fill that lack, to feel in the depths of your being, the emotions of love and loss that you and Cliff and Ben chose to experience his short life, knowing that by his passing you would all learn more in those few days than you had learned in centuries earlier."

"Stop it, Dad!" Beth exclaims. "You're talking nonsense.

I didn't know better, I'd say you were borderline senile. I asked you for clarification, not fantasy!"

Unfazed by Beth's outburst, her father goes on talking as though there had been no interruption. "Ben's decision to give you that experience, by the way, was an extraordinarily generous and loving one given that the most traumatic experience any earthbound soul will ever encounter is the birth experience. By that I mean the journey all souls wishing to become human must make through the birth canal. And he did that for your growth."

"Come on, Dad, give me a break!" Beth explodes throwing up her hands. "You can't expect me to believe a story like that! Besides, babies don't—can't—decide to die before they get born. Even grown-ups can't do that. Why would they? Everybody I know wants to live as long as they can. Except suicides, of course. I really thought you could do better than this. I'm disappointed."

"Sorry to disappoint you," her Dad replied, "but please remember he wasn't a baby at the time the decision was made. He was a fully cognizant, mature soul eager to be of assistance to you and Cliff whom he admired greatly. Also, if you'll remember, I told you that you made the decision in one life to live into your nineties and to depart your Beth life at age forty-six. Both decisions were made by you prior to your birth and not with the mind of an infant."

"You're still not making sense," Beth says with a sigh.

"Why..."

"Your Dad's doing his best," a voice behind her interrupts, "but maybe I can help him out."

Startled, Beth spins around to see a stooped, kindly looking man dressed in chinos and a faded denim shirt, smiling down at her. "I'm Zach," he says, grasping Beth by the shoulders and hugging her. "Feels real good to have you back. You did great this time out."

"How do you know what I did this time?" Beth snaps. "Are you someone I'm supposed to know?"

"You could say that," Zach says, the skin around his eyes crinkling with yet another smile. "Fact is, it's not just that you know me, it's that you're a part of me. Wherever you are, I am. I'm what you'd call your soul."

Hands on her hips, one foot tapping, Beth has listened to what this individual had to say with barely concealed scorn on her face.

"Great," she splutters, addressing her father. "I ask you for some good clear, logical explanation for what is going on and not only do you tell me a lot of drivel, but you sic this... This old windbag on me who tells me he's my soul! Give me a break! Souls aren't something you can see, for Pete's sake! They're invisible. Everybody knows that!"

"Now, honey," her father warns. "You need to listen to what Zach has to say. He is exactly what he says he is—your soul. It's not so much that he is a part of you as that you are a part of him. See, when a soul feels the need to experience a particular segment of human life for its own growth it sends out a fragment of itself to fulfill that need on the earth plane. In this case, Zach here, felt the need to experience the life of a woman juggling the roles of wife, mother and working woman in the tumult of the twentieth century."

"I don't believe any of this," Beth splutters, near tears again. "Instead of clarifying things for me, you're making everything horribly complicated, to say nothing of ridiculous. Are you telling me that I am—I was—an experiment, for God's sake? It's not true! I'm Beth Randall. Your daughter, remember? And I need to get out of this nightmare and back to my family right now. I ask you, I beg you, please help me do that."

"Beth," Zach interrupts, "Before we go any further, you need to understand, you must understand, that you have left behind forever the life you lived on earth as Beth Randall. You can observe it but not partake in it."

"I refuse to believe that," Beth replies, stamping her foot. "I'm standing here right now as Beth Randall. I'm talking to my father, who certainly knows I am Beth Randall. How dare you calmly say I'm not who I am?"

"Beth, Beth," Zach murmurs. "You are and always will *be* Beth Randall. Throughout eternity you will be Beth Randall. What I'm saying is that you have left the earth life you lived as her behind. You have returned to me, your soul, bringing with you a myriad of experiences and emotions that have greatly helped me enlarge my knowledge of humanity. After you have rested, after we have examined your Beth life in detail for triumphs and weaknesses, we will plan another adventure together so that we can continue to grow towards ever greater knowledge and understanding..."

"Don't talk to me about understanding," Beth snaps, "when it seems too difficult for either of you to understand that all I want to do is go home... And by that," she interrupts herself hastily, "I mean I want to go home to my family who must be worried sick by my absence. Is that so very hard to understand? They need me!"

"Let me show you something, Beth," Zach says, leading Beth back in the house and towards the recliner she had sat in to watch Ben's movie. "Have a seat and let me show you something. It will help clarify everything for you."

"Not another movie," Beth groans. "Please. I hated that last one! It had such an awful ending."

"This is a very short one, Beth," Zach reassures, "and it will clear everything up for you. You know, along the lines of a picture being worth a thousand words?"

"If I watch it, will you then help me find my way back where I belong?"

"Just watch it, honey," her father advises, sitting down beside her and taking her hand. "It really will help you understand what is happening."

"It better," Beth sighs. "Nothing anybody has said so far has made any kind of sense."

On the screen, Beth sees a procession of black limousines entering a cemetery. The cars come to a halt and their drivers assist the occupants in exiting the vehicles. Beth's eyes widen as she recognizes the people. They are her family. All of them dressed in black. A priest comes forward to greet them and escorts them into a small chapel. In front of the altar stands a coffin. Beth's family take their seats, all of them averting their eyes from the coffin but stealing sideways glances in spite of themselves.

Behind them the little chapel is packed with people, most of them in tears. To one side sits Mrs. James who looks on in disapproval. "I told her she'd never make it to Gainesville in time," she hisses audibly and self-righteously to Hilda who sits at her side. Hilda nods knowingly and with a sniff of disdain and in a loud voice, agrees, "Always in a hurry she was, that one. Always."

Overhearing these words, Beth's family collectively gasp in horror and, as much as they are able, turn their backs on the two old women.

The priest mounts the altar steps, prays silently for a moment, then turns to face the congregation, his arms raised. He makes the sign of the cross and an altar boy steps forward offering him a silver bowl containing holy water. The priest dips his fingers in the bowl and sprinkles the coffin, praying in Latin as he does so.

"Dearly beloved," he then intones, "we are gathered here today to remember and honor the life of Beth Randall, a devout Catholic, a devoted mother, a faithful wife and a staunch member of this parish, who was abruptly taken from this earth a few short days ago in a tragic traffic accident.

"Be that as it may, I know—we all know—that while we grievously lament our own personal loss, we must rejoice for Beth who is even now in the presence of our Lord and all his angels and saints who will have welcomed her to paradise with open arms, blaring trumpets and joyful choirs of celestial music."

Hearing these words, Beth turns to Zach with raised eyebrows and an I-told-you-so look on her face. Turning back to the service, Beth's face contorts at the unbridled grief the priest's words have on her family.

"I must go to them," she says, coming out of the recliner and addressing Zach. "They need to know I'm not dead. That I'm as alive as I've ever been. Please!"

Zach nods. Once again Beth hears the swooshing sound she heard earlier and with a gasp, realizes that she, together with Zach and her father, are now with the mourners in the chapel.

In two strides she is amongst her family. "Don't cry," she pleads. "Don't grieve. Look, see here, I'm with you. I'm not dead. It's all a mistake. That's not me in that coffin. How could it be when I'm here? Come on, let's

47

go home. We can... I can... I'll make us some lunch, a pot of coffee and... And together we'll get to the bottom of this whole... um... incident. Jane, I'm so sad I missed your graduation, honey. You looked so beautiful in your cap and gown. I... I saw you in the, um, parking lot."

No member of her family acknowledges her presence. Not Jane next to whom she stands. Not Jimmy and Betsy who cling to one another in abject misery. Not Cliff who, face wet with tears, gropes in his pockets for a non-existent handkerchief.

"See what happens when I'm not there to lay your clothes out for you," Beth half-jokingly chides, hoping for a smile.

When she gets no reaction she turns to the congregation in general. "Go home, all of you" she calls. "It's not true that I died. It's all a mistake. I'm here. Look at me!"

The mourners do not look up from their hymnals. Beth strides towards Mrs. James and attempts to snatch her hymnal from her hands.

"You're wasting your time," Zach murmurs. "We're in a different dimension now. Nothing you can do from our side will affect them."

Beth turns away in exasperation and addresses her father. "Can't you get through to any of them? I mean, come on! They're your family, too, you know."

Her father shakes his head. "Honey," he begins, "If I could, I would. You should have seen me trying to get through to you and the others at my own funeral. But they can't see you or hear you. As Zach said, we're in different dimensions."

"If either of you would only stop to think about it," Zach says testily, "you'd realize how unsettling it would be for them to see you at your own funeral. Think about it. They saw the photos of the accident, identified your body at the morgue, made all the funeral arrangements and now you want to pay them a surprise visit? Come on, give them a break."

"How about somebody gives me a break?" Beth snaps. "How do you think I feel not being able to communicate with my own family. Them all thinking I'm dead. Me stuck in this kind of limbo where everybody *is* dead. Where nothing makes any kind of sense. And where nobody will tell me what to do to get out of it." Once again she starts to cry.

"The first thing you have to do, Beth," Zach tells her, "is accept the situation you're in."

"I'll never do that," Beth gasps. "What, just up and abandon everybody? Everything I've lived for? How could I? They all need me. And I still have so much to do."

"Believe me, Beth," Zach said, "You were finished there. You did everything you set out to do at the beginning. You learned the lessons you went to learn and I can't thank you enough for the insights I gained through you in that life."

As Zach speaks these last words, the congregation

gets up from their knees, pall bearers step forward and lift the coffin off the trestle on which it has rested and slowly proceed with it to the front door of the chapel. The congregation falls into a ragged line behind them. Beth, her father, and Zachary follow the mourners to the grave site.

Beth sobs out loud as her coffin is lowered into the ground and family members step forward in turn to sprinkle a small amount of earth on top of it with a hand-held, silver shovel. "I can't believe that's the end of me," she sniffles.

"It's not the end of you, you big silly," Zach says, trying hard to be patient, "just the end of that particular, physical body. You can see for yourself you will always retain the body you are in now. Your astral body. Look at me. Read my lips. You are not dead. You will never die. You are eternal."

"The end of that particular body," Beth mimics. "Well, for your information, Oh, Great Soul, I liked that particular body and I don't like seeing it buried. Fact is, I feel like I got cheated having to leave so soon."

"That was your decision, way back when," Zach reminds her.

"I know, I know. Dad told me about it. But now I realize I could have gone on another twenty, thirty years. I liked being Beth. It was a nice life."

"I did, too," Zach agreed. "It was one of our better outings but, don't worry, we'll have many more. And as you open your mind to greater truths, and begin to see everything in its proper perspective, you'll understand and appreciate all the other reasons you decided to depart when you did."

"Many more?" Beth repeats with a gulp. "Many more what?"

"Lives," Zach answers with a grin. "What else. That's what it's all about, learning... growing... and eventually, when you choose, going beyond time and space. We've still got lots to do, we two. But with the knowledge and experience we just gained as Beth, we should really be able to make great strides in the next one. Oh, and by the way, nice to see you are starting to accept your situation. It helps us move forward."

"Move forward?" Beth queries faintly, her face mirroring the question marks in her voice. "To what?"

"To higher and higher levels of understanding. And as we learn here so, in our next incarnation, we will be able to bring more knowledge with us until we ultimately become what is known as a Master, meaning one with full knowledge of the power that is available to all, always and forever."

"That sounds almost sacrilegious to me," Beth says uneasily. "The nuns at the Sacred Heart would flay you alive hearing you talk like that. You'd be doing penance and saying rosaries for the rest of your life. That is, if you ever had a life, I mean."

"Yeah, well," Zach shrugs, "Being a nun or a priest

doesn't mean they know all the answers. They're mortal too, you know. Learning like everyone else."

"I don't know," Beth murmurs. "I always thought nuns and priests were just kind of born holier than the rest of us; that by living the way they do they're less tempted to break the commandments, can maybe pull off a miracle or two and then go straight to heaven, no questions asked."

"Everyone goes to heaven," Zach replies. "Besides, there are countless, non-religious souls living on earth right now who quietly perform miracles every day."

"Not in this day and age they don't," Beth protests sharply. "Are you kidding me? With CNN and all the other media out there, the news would flash around the world in seconds."

"Not necessarily," Zach answers. "There are miracles going on every day on earth that don't get any attention because those who perform them don't even realize what they are doing. They just think they were in the right place at the right time.

"Then too, little miracles happen every day in people's lives and they're just too busy, too preoccupied, to recognize them for what they are."

"Like what?"

"Like you're driving out in the country and you miss a turn. It's getting dark, starting to snow and BAM, you've got a flat. There's no spare in the trunk. You're desperate. Half an hour goes by. And then you see headlights coming towards you. You jump out of your car, wave for assistance. The car pulls up and guess what? The driver is an old friend of yours. Someone you hadn't seen since high school. He has a spare. He changes your tire. Says, "The darndest thing is, Beth, you'd been on my mind this last hour or so. You just moved in out of nowhere. And then I got an urge to go out and take a look around and... here you are! What gives?"

"Nowadays, they call things like that serendipities," Beth interrupts, barely masking a sneer.

"Call them anything you want. Fact is, they're miracles."

"Not in my book, they're not. I'd say I got lucky, that's all."

"I'd say you got more than lucky," Zach growls, "I'd say..."

"Enough!" Beth snaps. "You want to call it a miracle, go ahead. What I want to do is get back to me and you. Us. In the first place, I want to know how and why I got to be Beth and then... Well... let's just start there."

"OK, OK," Zach says, shaking his head at her stubborn attitude. He nods towards Beth's Dad who is stretched out on the couch sound asleep. "Let's go back out by the pool, let your Dad enjoy his nap."

With a start Beth realizes that unaccountably they are no longer at her funeral service but back in what Ben had called her dream home.

Taking Beth's arm, Zach steers her to the end of the pool deck where he unlatches a small gate in a dense hedge. Beth gasps at the unexpected loveliness spread out before her. From a flagstone terrace, steps lead down to an emerald green lawn surrounded by deep, flowering borders stretching to a shimmering lake. At various intervals, giant stands of oaks provide shade and inviting seating areas.

"This is just like a garden I once saw on a tour of stately homes in England," she marvels.

"It is," Zach smiles. "From the moment you first saw it, you could think of nothing else. You craved it, imagined yourself enjoying it and, like all the other things you thought you could never attain, you filed it in the back of your mind as a 'Some day...' kind of thing. Something to strive toward."

"Didn't do me much good, did it?" Beth says, with a touch of bitterness. "All that striving, I mean. I didn't come close to achieving this or any of the other beautiful things back there in the house."

"Did you ever wonder why?" Zach asks.

"You bet I did," Beth says hotly. "I could never understand it. Used to drive me crazy. I worked hard, Cliff worked harder. We made a lot of money and yet... all the really beautiful things seemed forever out of reach. That, or they fell into the hands of the Mrs. Jameses of the world. Made me sick sometimes."

"You didn't get them because your thoughts dwelled

on the lack of them, their absence," Zach says. "And rather indignantly, I might add. You had an 'It's not fair,' attitude. If your thoughts had dwelt instead on enjoying them, using them on a day to day basis, they would have been yours."

"Yeah, right," Beth says sarcastically. "And where, might I ask, would they have come from?"

"You. You would have given them to yourself. Stop and think about it for a moment. Who gave you all the things you did have back there on earth? The home, the cars, the clothes, the abundance?"

"Why... I don't know," Beth says, studying Zach carefully. "I mean, I guess I thought if whatever it was was a necessity then I went ahead and bought it."

"And didn't you, once in a while, shall we say, acquire, something you didn't think was a necessity?" Zach asks, with a knowing smile. "Come on, think about it. That Persian rug in your entry hall, for example? The Cartier watch? The SUV?"

"Well... Yes... I did splurge occasionally. I thought I deserved a break once in a while. So what?"

"So in other words you gave them to yourself. I mean, a fairy godmother didn't appear out of the bushes and grant you three wishes or anything like that, did she?"

Beth rolls her eyes in exasperation. "No, a fairy godmother did not appear and shower me with gifts. I went out and bought them myself. Again, so what?"

"We've come full circle," Zach says. "Everything you

really, really wanted, thought you couldn't live without, you gave to yourself, that's what. Now, tell me, why did you stop? Giving to yourself, I mean."

Now Beth is thoroughly exasperated. "Look," she says, "this conversation is leading us nowhere. I didn't give myself more because I thought I couldn't afford it. Thought it was wrong to be so hung up on status symbols; thought I was being greedy wanting so much while others had so little. Besides, we're not *there* anymore, are we? We're *here*. So what's the point?"

"The point," Zach says, "a point I might add, that you failed to notice either on earth or here, is that in every sentence you or I have uttered, thought comes into the equation. You *thought* you deserved this or that. You *thought* you'd be seen as greedy if you acquired the other." He looks at Beth questioningly. She shrugs, spreads her hands.

"Let's move away from possessions and toward other facets of your Beth life," Zach goes on. "Let's look at the morning of Jane's graduation.'

Involuntarily Beth shudders, shakes her head. "Please, let's not," she says. "It's still too painful to even think about."

"We won't dwell on the end of the day," Zach assures her. "We'll just go through the early hours, OK? You worried, you *thought*, Cliff would get too involved in his golf and be late. You *thought* the other kids would be late. You *thought*, Mrs. James would delay you. You *thought* your daughter and daughter-in-law would dress inappropriately."

"Enough!" Beth snaps, putting her hands up to her ears. "What are you getting at? My family has always been like that. I have to do their thinking for them or nothing ever gets done."

"Exactly," Zach says. "And so nothing ever got done. Have I made my point?"

"No," Beth spits. "Nothing you've said since I met you has made any sense. If you really are my soul then all I can say is you're a big disappointment. I would have expected kindly words of wisdom from my soul, not an old windbag that talks in riddles."

Zach shakes his head, smiles, "Guess I've been called worse," he shrugs. "Let's start over."

"No," Beth exclaims, "I... I've had enough. We came out here to talk about me, my Beth life, and then you got sidetracked."

"We were—are—talking about your Beth life, and we've also touched on some of your other lives as well," Zach says. "And the one thing they all have in common, that every life ever lived has in common, is the function of thought. This is one of your lessons. It's something everyone has to learn."

"Let's not go back to that again, please. I don't see what thought has to do with anything," Beth groans.

"People think. Me, just like everybody else. But it's not telling me a thing about my life as Beth and that's what I want to hear from you now."

"OK, OK," Zach says. "Back to your life as Beth and how or why we chose it. But just so you know, sooner or later, we will have to get back to thought. It's key to everything, past, present and future."

"We'll make it later," Beth murmurs. "Much later."

Again, Zach leading the way, Beth following, they return to the flagstone terrace where they take seats and Zach begins.

"You won't remember—you will, but not yet—that we once chose a life in Italy where you were the impoverished, overworked wife of a drunken, brutal farmer. You gave birth to twelve kids, miscarried two more. We both agreed we wouldn't want to go that route again. The hunger, the frustration, the exhaustion, the pain. It was so relentless."

Beth, eyes wide in horror, nods mutely.

"After your Italian experience," Zach continues, "you decided not to live as a woman for a long, long time and, after a good rest, you had a couple of nice, easy lives as a male."

Beth, who had been lazily admiring the way the sun reflected on the water of the pool, comes upright in her chair, mouth agape. "As a guy?" she gasps.

"Yes, a guy." Zach says with a smile. "Don't look so

amazed. Over the centuries you've been male many times."

"But, it's not possible," Beth argues. "Me? Male? I don't believe you! I'd never choose to be male. They're so..."

"Trust me, in those last two you were an exemplary male. Kind. Considerate. An excellent father."

"A father? Me?"

"Yes, you. In fact in one of them you were Cliff's father."

"No way! That sounds indecent. Incestuous. I couldn't have been."

"Take it from me, you were. Remember how the day you met him as Beth, you thought there was something familiar about him? Something endearing. Well, now you know why. Try not to be shocked when I tell you he was also your sister in another life way back in the middle ages."

Beth is speechless as she stares at Zach who is studying her with a kindly smile. "Tell me," she begins slowly, "just how many lives have I shared with Cliff?"

"A good dozen as best I can remember."

"A dozen, huh? How about the other members of my family? The family I just left, I mean. Were they in any of them?"

"Some were, some are more recent. Way back in what you'd call pre-historic times, you hung around with a whole different family—in inter-changeable roles, of course—a good twenty lifetimes. A couple of them joined you again in your Beth family."

"Twenty lifetimes?"

"Yes. But remember, back then a life only lasted twenty, thirty years or so. Those were very tough years for the race. It was all about survival. Think, they didn't even have the wheel back then."

"I can only imagine," Beth says faintly, coming to her feet. "I think... That is... I don't think I want to listen to anymore of this. It's all so far out. Outrageously so. I'd like to... I mean, I think I'd like to be by myself for a while now.

"And so you shall," Zach agrees. "We'll just spend a couple more minutes going over your life as Beth and then you can have some quiet time."

Dazedly, Beth agrees and sits back down.

"We took it on—her on," Zach begins, "for a couple of reasons. One, it still rankled with you that you had allowed yourself to be so down-trodden in the Italian life where not just you but all women were treated little better than cattle. You felt you had to prove that women could do more than just bear children; show that they had fine creative minds if only given the chance.

"And secondly, you wanted to indulge yourself with a life that would afford you time to enjoy all the marvels that life can offer. For that reason, you wanted to be able to have a job—a career—that would afford you an income of your own, while at the same time having a husband and becoming a mother," his eyes twinkle, "though not of twelve!"

Beth nods emphatically.

"In short, you wanted an "easy" life," Zach goes on. "That is, an abundant life with no shortage of money, no deformities, no diseases. You wanted every comfort, modern appliances, cars instead of donkeys...

"Together we decided on the United States as the best place to live such a life because of the high standard of living there and because more and more women there were convinced, like you, they could do and have it all.

"We decided that this time around you would be a white woman and we chose your Mom and Dad as the best candidates. They agreed because they wanted another child, a girl. And since they were a handsome pair they knew you'd inherit the good looks you insisted upon."

"Look," Beth interrupts, "I know you mean well and you're just doing your job but you've got my head spinning with all these lives you say I've lived. I mean, male, female. And you say I chose white this time? Are you inferring I was black in another?"

Zach nods. "Yep, many times. And all shades in between."

"Wait. Don't say another word until you tell me one important thing. Why do we—all humans—choose to live all these lives anyway? What's the point?"

"To learn. To know. To truly understand every facet

of the human condition, including painful, ugly and cruel, so that through empathy and compassion, love can blossom in ways not otherwise possible.

"By the same token, there is the beauty of life to appreciate. The marvels of nature and the ingenuity of man. The literature, music, art, architecture, cuisine, the wonders of medicine, extraordinary inventions and, most wonderful of all, the exhilaration of seeing something come into being and knowing that you created it through your thoughts."

"I still don't get it," Beth says with a scowl. "So we learn. We create. But surely there's a better way. This just all seems so cruel to me. Aren't there ever any nice, easy, beautiful lives?"

"Of course. And most are. You just lived one, remember? As to why we do it again and again? Surely you must see from what I just told you about the variety of lives, that it would not be possible to experience all there is to know in any one lifetime. The body wears out. You tried that in your 90-odd year life and it was too much for you.

"The reason we live so many different lives is for the understanding each one brings. It's one thing to observe—talk about, theorize—different ways of life, feel pity for those who suffer because of discrimination, poverty, religion. But until you actually live such lives yourself you will never, ever truly understand.

"One of the hardest things for mortals to learn is

to be non-judgmental. Only by living through painful circumstances themselves can they begin to understand the depths to which a soul can sink and learn not to judge those who are uneducated, brutal, unkind. Those who steal, lie, cheat, even murder."

"It's not hard now to see why being Beth was such a breeze," Beth says with a shudder. "So, tell me, what of value, what gems of wisdom, did we learn by being Beth?"

"The life of Beth became a driven life. You wanted to be perfect in everything you attempted. You thought yourself invincible and anything that got in your way had to be pushed aside, buried. Consequently, in striving for perfection in all areas you allowed little time to feel your emotions. You buried them. You were too busy.

"For you to know, emotion is the most valuable prize mortals bring to their over-souls. In fact, emotion can only be experienced fully, through the five senses, whilst in the human form. In concentrating almost solely on your ambitions, you basically ignored the wants and needs of others. In living this with you I gained a better understanding of the single-minded individual." He grimaces, shrugs. "And now they have my sympathy and understanding. They'll have yours, too, when you are ready for a thorough life review."

"That's not what you said when I first got here," Beth says hotly. "Then you said I'd done a great job. Or something to that effect."

"You did well in many areas," Zach says soothingly. "Just not necessarily through your career phase. It dominated you. Everyone got short changed in that area, none more so than you.

"The really big prize you brought back with you this time around were the torrents of emotions brought about by Ben's arrival and departure. In that brief little life of his he taught the most valuable lesson of all. All of you learned the true value and meaning of emotion, most particularly the emotion of love.

"You see, we did have one other female lifetime after the Italian episode. It was at the turn of the century. You were a wealthy, titled woman in England. In those days, in the circles in which you moved, children were considered little more than messy, noisy nuisances. They were to be seen and not heard. At birth, they were put in the care of various nannies, many of whom were unsatisfactory, and as soon as humanly possible, they were packed off to boarding schools. Following that, if they were females they were quickly married off and if male, a stint in the military was considered a useful way to spend their days until they would inherit the title and the wealth.

"It should be obvious from what I've said, that the notion of love would have been considered a weakness. Something to be kept to oneself with a stiff upper lip. Life in those days was all about duty. All sentiment was denied and seen as "sissy."

"The entity we now know as Ben was such a child. He was your child."

"I can't bear to think of it," Beth shudders, her eyes filling with tears. "It's too awful. The poor little darling. But I see what you're getting at. This time around he did all that he set out to do. Broke through not only the masks Cliff and I lived behind, but entered our hearts. He taught us what it is to really appreciate a child. Not only that, but to let go. In just two days he did all that."

"He did indeed," Zach says, coming to his feet. "And in many ways, your passing as Beth, under the circumstances chosen, will serve Cliff and all those you loved.

"And now, time for you to take that nice long rest I've been promising. Follow me."

Following behind Zach through the dream house, Beth sees and marvels at many more beautiful rooms, each one decorated with things she had once admired and longed for.

Shaking her head at the wonder and beauty of it all, she gasps when Zach stops at double doors and throws them open.

"Your room, madam," he says, with a mock bow. "I believe you'll find everything your heart ever desired within easy reach."

"Why... This is every woman's dream bedroom," Beth

gasps, her eyes feasting on every detail. "I love it."

"Enjoy," Zach says, preparing to close the door.

"Wait!" Beth says hastily, "You will... I mean, we will resume this conversation soon, won't we? It seems the more you tell me, the more questions I have. I've gone from not wanting to hear any of it to wanting to hear all of it."

"You only have to think of me and I'll be with you instantly," Zach reassures.

"That's one of the things I really need you to explain," Beth says, her head coming up sharply. "This thinking... thought... business. You seem to give it so much importance and even Ben mentioned it earlier."

"We'll get to it all, trust me," Zach says with a wink. "Relax now and when you're ready, we'll take up where we left off."

Alone for the first time since she met up with Ben—when was it, minutes... hours... days ago?—Beth exhales loudly, and flops down on the bed, her mind whirling with all she'd seen and heard since arriving in this strange but magnificent place. Ben. Her parents. Zach. The movie of her life. The one of her funeral. The many, many lives she supposedly lived both as male and female. It was all too much. She still had no clear idea of where she was and for the moment it didn't seem to matter. Stretching out with a contented sigh on linens that smelled faintly of lavender, Beth smiled as she remembered the words she'd heard so often since her arrival. Words she was beginning to like. "You've got all the time in the world now, Beth."

What a wonderful way to go on living—maybe "being" would be a better word?—she thought drowsily, with all the time in the world. I think I'm going to really love being here.

One More Time

Pete lives in a magnificent home. Gardens that rival those of the Palace of Versailles surround his estate. Everything Pete ever imagined, he has. And since he has a very vivid imagination his house is crammed with wondrous artifacts from every corner of the earth.

Pete is also fascinated by gadgets, particularly those of the electronic variety. Over time he has accumulated such an assortment that he had to have a special wing built on to his house to accommodate them all.

Musical instruments are another favorite of his but... I won't go into them just now or we'll be here all day.

Before we go any further, I should tell you that Pete is an angel. Not that you'd ever know it to look at him. Not for him the usual angel attire of flowing white robes, halos and harps although, being the avid collector he is, he does own all of those things. He keeps them in a special walk-in closet in his bedroom. The white robes are carefully hung and covered with tissue paper, the harp resides in a leather case embossed with his initials and his halos—he has several in varying widths—rest on racks above the robes.

But as I said, Pete rarely, if ever, wears his angel garb, preferring, instead, what he sees being worn on earth. He's always had an eye for what's "in," has our Pete, and since he goes back and forth a lot—especially lately—he's taken a liking to "grunge." By this I mean he's grown a goatee of sorts, let his hair grow shaggy, and is most comfortable in jeans and sneakers.

His boss, Gabe—aka The Archangel Gabriel—has gone along with most of Pete's fashion whims. He's even adopted a few of them himself over time. But he put his foot down firmly on blue jeans. "White jeans," he said, "are OK. But the blue ones have to go."

"Aw, c'mon, man," Pete argued. "Everyone's wearing them over there. Men, women, kids. I'd blow my cover if I show up over there dressed, like... you know..."

But Gabriel was adamant. "White jeans or the robe," he said. "Take your pick."

So... Pete wears the white ones. To keep up the grunge look, though, he lets them get plenty dirty and when he sends them out to be washed, he insists on no bleach.

As you can imagine, angels have many responsibilities and Pete is no exception. On the "heaven" side of the equation, angels spend a lot of time in choir practice and in greeting returning souls from earth and making them comfortable. On the "earth" side, they meet newly arriving souls and help them adjust to the ways of the world—especially the noise factor, which can be brutal to a newborn. And every once in a while they'll step in—albeit reluctantly—to provide a miracle or two, but only when absolutely necessary. All in all then, being an angel is busy work but no one could call it hard work.

Now, in spite of what could rightly be called an idyllic existence by any standard, Pete is not a happy angel. Pete has a problem. A problem who goes by the name of Celeste. Celeste not only drives Pete crazy on a daily basis—and has for centuries—but, more importantly, her recalcitrant behavior is keeping him from a long overdue promotion to the Seventh Heaven.

It is Pete's present responsibility to escort Celeste back to earth for one final incarnation. Not a whole lengthy cycle of lives, mind, but just one teeny-tiny solitary little life, and Celeste refuses to go.

He's entreated, cajoled and even threatened, but nothing he's said so far has convinced her. Celeste is as determined to stay right where she is as Pete is for her to go.

At his wits end, Pete even went so far as to ask Gabriel himself to come over to his house tonight to help convince her, and we all know you don't bother an illustrious angel like Gabriel with trivia. But during his most recent conversation with Celeste, Pete was able to persuade her to stop by after dinner, feeling certain that with Gabe at his side—Gabe with his air of authority, his gifts of empathy, oratory and love—Celeste would finally see the light.

Right now, though, Celeste is late and Pete is beside

himself, behaving, I'm sorry to say, in many ways more like a human than an angel. He pauses in his pacing. Was that a knock on his door? He hurries towards it, opens it wide, and... in walks Gabe.

"Man, am I ever glad to see you," Pete says. "Thanks for coming."

"Relax, Pete," Gabe soothes. "I said I'd show."

"I know it. Still... something could have come up. Something more important."

"What could be more important than seeing you get promoted. You're way overdue."

Pete groans, rubs his fingers through his chin stubble. "Tell me about it! I swear she stalls on me this time, I'll... I don't know what I'll do. I can't take much more of this place."

"She's not going to stall on you. I'll make her change her mind. Never met a soul yet I couldn't convince. How do you think I earned my title, huh?

So go ahead, bring her on."

Pete gulps, massages his stubble again, avoids Gabe's eyes. "See... the thing is," he mumbles, "uh... she hasn't shown. And only yesterday when I talked to her she said—she promised—she'd come by."

It's clear both from his face and body language that Gabe is not pleased. He is, after all a very busy angel with souls of his own to deal with and a myriad other duties. Besides, he's just itching to install the new software he ordered into his PC.

"Look, Pete," he begins, trying not to sound too irate, "I've gone out of my way to get here but it's open house at my place tonight and you know how that goes. Rooms full of souls waiting on me. I mean, you're my man and I want to help, but c'mon, it's not up to me to get them in the door. That's your job."

"I know it, man," Pete moans, "and I'm sorry. I never would have wasted your time if I thought she wasn't gonna show."

He gestures towards a brightly illuminated building on the other side of his vast lawn, which is actually the spot where heaven ends and earth begins. "They're all there, he says. "The others... Been at it a good couple hours already."

Gabe glances towards the building Pete has indicated, shrugs his shoulder, "Yeah," he says, "well, we all know these things take time over there. Why don't you try calling her?"

Pete yanks his cell phone out of his jeans' pocket—his white jeans pocket—punches in numbers, paces, listens, shrugs.

Scowling, he slams the phone shut, walks to the front door, opens it and yells, "Celeste! You out there? Celeste?"

He lingers a while, peering into the darkness, then slams the door shut. Turning to Gabe, shaking his head in disgust, he says, "Hey, I'm really sorry about this. I swear I had her convinced."

Gabe makes his way to a comfortable armchair, sinks into it with a sigh, "From the look of things over there," he indicates the building across the lawn where the silhouettes of several people can be seen scurrying around the lower floor, "they've still got a ways to go. We could..."

A faint sound interrupts him and both angels turn towards the direction it came from. They see the front door slowly opening and an untidy, harried-looking woman of indeterminate age enters tentatively. She closes the door behind her and leans against it, one hand clutching the knob.

"Celeste!" Pete exclaims, hurrying forward to greet her. "You made it! Boy, am I ever glad to see you! Come in, come in." He reaches for her hands to bring her into the room but Celeste keeps them firmly behind her back.

"I just stopped by... to tell you..." Celeste begins, her hand tightening on the doorknob, "I... I'm not going..."

"You don't know what you're saying, baby," Pete says. "'Course you're going. You got to. Isn't anybody else can go but you. Tell her, Gabe!"

Gabe pulls himself out of his chair, walks slowly towards Celeste who presses herself ever more firmly against the door.

"Pete's right, Celeste," he says gently. "This is your time, honey. Go make it count!"

Celeste's lower lip juts out, she adopts a more

belligerent stance, "I said I'm not going," she growls.

Pete motions to her, pats the seat of an armchair invitingly, "Come on over here have a seat, Sweetie," he says. "Let's talk it over."

Celeste takes a step forward into the room but goes no further. "Talk all you want," she says with a toss of her head. "It's not going to change anything."

"Hey," Pete says, suddenly remembering his manners, "Want you to meet my buddy Gabe here. He was just over there. Says they've got stuff going on now you won't believe. Wait'll you hear."

Celeste turns towards Gabe with a questioning look. "Don't I know you from somewhere?" she begins, then shrugs. "Don't matter. Nothing you or anybody else says is gonna make me change my mind."

"Celeste," Pete groans. "You don't know what you're saying. It's this whole computer thing."

"I know computers," Celeste spits. "Jeez, they've been around for eons! I was a programmer last time out, remember?"

"Not like now, they haven't," Pete argues. "They got computers now that can drive cars, make out shopping lists on what's low in your refrigerator, tell you how to get where you want to go. I mean, between us angels and computers it's getting so people don't have to figure out nothing no more. Us and the computers do it all for them."

"'Bout time, too," Celeste snorts. "Never met a person

yet who could figure out stuff for themselves. That's how come I like it here so much. No computers. No time. No CNN. No money. No sweat!"

"C'mon Celeste," Pete sighs. "You know there's more than this for both of us."

"Speak for yourself," Celeste says with a toss of her head. "I've never been happier than where I am right now."

Gabe strolls forward to within a few feet of Celeste, gives her his most beatific smile. "Give him a break, honey," he urges. "He's worked with you going on centuries. He has to send in another, 'No progress' he gets another, 'No progress.' Is that what you want? Both of you stuck here in this limbo forever?"

"Wouldn't worry me none," Celeste says, "I like everything here. Feels like," she giggles, "feels like I died and went to heaven."

Pete turns away in disgust, "Know what, Celeste? I've had it with you. You back out on me this time I'm gonna ask The Man to get you a new celestial host."

"Yeah?" Celeste sneers, "Maybe I'd of had a different celestial host from the start I'd be done already. You ever think about that?"

"How about if I'd had a different soul?" Pete explodes. "I'd have me a corner office on the seventh floor by now. A whole new set of wings and halos, maybe. You're the one keeping me back!"

Gabe steps forward, places himself between them.

"Come on you two," he says. "Getting personal isn't going to help. Celeste, all he's asking is one more go-round. You'll be back before you know it."

"He's right, Celeste," Pete says, speaking now in a much calmer voice. "You're nearly there. Just a couple loose ends to tie up and that's it. You're home for good."

"No kidding," Celeste's voice oozes sarcasm. "So what did I forget last time? To let the cat out?"

"That and a couple other things," Pete begins,
"Like..."

"Forget it!" Celeste growls. "I'm not going!"

Gabe's face takes on a more serious look. "Celeste," he begins, "you know how this works same as us. You've got to go back one more time. There's no way around it."

"You're wrong there, buddy." Celeste snaps. "I'm a creature of free will, remember?"

"I don't get you," Gabe says, turning away in disgust. "You know as well as me that you don't have to stay forever. Return tickets are always part of the deal."

"It's not the return I'm worried about," Celeste snarls. "It's the going that freaks me out. Going through the birth canal... Being a helpless infant again... You tried it just once you'd see what I mean. It's the worst. The pits!"

"See what I mean," Pete says to Gabe. "She don't listen."

"You wouldn't either if you were a woman," Celeste exclaims. "It's tough going over there a woman. Alone..."

"You've never been there alone," Pete howls. "Never! I've been with you every single life!"

"Yeah, right. That's what you always say. Here. But when I'm over there and I need you, where are you? Nowhere I ever saw."

"Yeah?" Pete sneers. "How about last time out in Italy and you were dumb enough to get in a stranger's car at two o'clock in the morning, huh?"

"I had to," Celeste snaps. "I missed the last bus. You think I was going to stand around in the freezing cold and the pouring rain till 6 a.m.?"

"Got scary though, didn't it," Pete says, "the guy's hand going up under your skirt?"

"Yeah, it got scary. Just like everything else over there is scary."

"Lucky for you that car you were riding in got rear-ended at a traffic light, huh?" Pete sneers.

"Yeah, it was. Jeez, that hadn't happened I could've got raped. Strangled with my panty hose!"

"And lucky for you," Gabe interjects, "a cab pulled up right then and you grabbed it while Romeo was screaming obscenities, huh?"

"Tell me about it," Celeste gulps, remembering. "Must've been my lucky day." She pauses, frowns,

"Hey, how come you two know so much about that incident?"

"Who do you think was driving the car that rear-ended you?" Pete asks.

"Who do you think was driving the cab?" Gabe asks.

"That's how come I know you," Celeste gasps, looking at Gabe. "I recognized your voice. But... Come on. You guys are spooking me. What gives?"

"Just part of the job," Gabe smiles. "Looking out for souls that get lost like you."

"Still think you're on your own over there?" Pete asks.

"I just don't get it," Celeste says, shaking her head. "What's with the game playing? The dumb disguises?"

Gabe's face takes on a pious look. "Part of the fun is working in mysterious ways our wonders to unfold," he intones.

Celeste plops herself down in an armchair. "Forget the wonders," she spits. "It's thinking about times like that—and a bunch of others—make me know I don't want to go back. That, and the everlasting worry about money. Earning it. Keeping it. Losing it. Plus getting the *good* education. The *right* career. A kind husband. Then along comes the kids. The messed-up relationships. No thanks! Been there, done that way too many times already."

Gabe turns to Pete. "You're right," he says with an air of finality. "You're never going to get the office on the seventh floor and all the bells and whistles working with this one. Just tell The Man you'll trade her for a couple brand new souls and give her up."

"But..." Pete gulps, "I can't give up on her now. I've worked too hard and... she's so close!"

"With an attitude like hers?" Gabe scowls, "I don't think so. Too bad, though. I mean, it's not like anyone else can do it, is it? She'll just have to..."

"What do you mean nobody else can do it?" Celeste asks, coming to her feet. "There's a ton of souls over here just itching to go back!"

"So?" Gabe says. "None of them are you, are they?"

"So?" Celeste snaps back. "Doesn't mean they can't do the same things I do, does it?"

"Celeste, Celeste," Gabe says with a long suffering sigh. "You've been around long enough to know there's nobody in the entire world just exactly like you. You're one of a kind."

Celeste preens. "Now you're making me feel kind of special," she simpers.

"I swear," Pete gasps. "I've been telling you that since day one."

"Not like he just did," Celeste argues. "You never told me I was, like, 'One of a kind'."

"You've got eyes, haven't you?" Pete says. "You ever see any duplicates over there? That's why you got to go do it your way. You don't, there'll be a piece of the puzzle forever missing—Celeste's way!"

"Wow!" Celeste gasps. "I never knew I was that important!"

"Oh, and by the way, Celeste," Gabe says, as though suddenly remembering something. "Someone over there right now needs you real bad."

"Me? Why would anybody need me?"

"We just got done telling you," Pete groans. "'Cause you're you. Remember Tilly, that pal of yours from back in... let's see... must have been your Irish incarnation?"

"'Course I remember Tilly!" Celeste says, her face lighting up. "Silly Tilly I used to call her. Best friend I ever had. She's the one got me and my kids through the famine. Brought us food. Even helped us immigrate. She's there?"

"She's there," Gabe answers. "Been there going on a year already. Only, see, she's not welcome. Her mother this time around wanted a boy and when Tilly showed up the woman wouldn't even look at her. Hides her in a back room. Mistreats her. Even dropped her once. Kid never has seen the light of day. She needs someone like you, tough, strong, opinionated to get her through, see she gets to live the whole long life she planned."

"Oh-h-h-h," Celeste moans. "That's so sad. My poor Tilly. But... what can I do?"

"Show up! Be the boy the woman has always wanted. The big brother Tilly is going to need her whole life."

Celeste's mouth drops open. "Well... Yeah... Sure... But... Be a guy again? I mean..."

"You can do it," Gabe reassures. "You did great last time you were a guy, remember?"

"Yeah, but that was a good dozen lifetimes ago!"

"Doesn't matter. It will all come back to you, you know that. Besides, you just got done complaining about how hard it is to be a woman. And with Tilly in the picture to take care of, you'll have your hands way too full to get into any of those macho male hang-ups you got bogged down in last time."

"Yeah, but Tilly's never gonna know it's me."

"Not till the end, she won't, but that's not what is important. What's important is she'll sense a certain familiarity, have confidence that with you around to turn to, she'll always be safe. And that's a pretty darn nice way to live a life, feeling safe."

"You're the only one can do it, Celeste," Pete reminds her. "Remember that."

"And another thing," Gabe reminds her. "You help Tilly through this, you help Pete here and you help yourself."

"OK. OK. Enough already!" Celeste says, putting her hands over her ears. "Forget Pete and me. It's Tilly I'm thinking about now. I'd have known it was her needing me, I'd have gone sooner. Is everything, like, ready?"

Gabe and Pete stand to peer through the night at the building across the way where frantic activity is now taking place. They give each other a thumbs up.

"They're ready." Pete says. "Been ready so long

they've about given up on you. You're gonna love this life, Celeste."

Celeste gulps. "You're sure about that?"

"'Course we're sure. You've always loved Tilly. Always loved New York. What's not to be sure about?"

"She's in New York?" Celeste gasps, a radiant smile lighting up her face. "Al-right! I'm on my way. Quick, what's my purpose this time? I mean, apart from helping Tilly."

"Same as always, Celeste," Gabe says. "Love."

"Love 'em all, Celeste," Pete adds. "Every last one. And get it right this time, OK? Start by learning to love yourself first. Work at it. Then the rest'll come easy."

"I will! I will!" Celeste calls. "And this time I swear I'm gonna get it right so when I get to come back, I'll be home for good!"

"Go then!" Gabe commands. "And peace be with you. And all the other holy, holy stuff."

"I'm on my way. I love you guys!"

"Then you're off to a good start!"

Celeste waves and blows kisses. Pete and Gabe watch as her vapor trails across the lawn and enters earth.

Both angels dive for the intercom, turn up the volume just in time to hear the first lusty roar of a newborn.

"She did it! She's there!" Pete exults, giving Gabe a high five.

"She sure is," Gabe agrees. "And so are you, old guy. From now on you're gonna be flying high with us archangels.

The End of the Line

Seems like the older I gets, the slower time moves and wouldn't you think, settin' at the wheel of a city bus mindin' out for trucks, amb'lances, taxis and pedestrians wantin' to jump in every crosswalk before ever I gets my bus to a stop, wouldn't you think with all that goin' on every second, the hours'd fly by like minutes?

Don't happen. Leastways, not no more it don't. Used to be a time it did. Used to be the hours went by so fast I never could figure where they went.

'Course that was all of forty years ago. Yep. Forty years I been drivin' for the City of Atlanta and every one of 'em accident free. Leastways, while I been in my share of accidents, wasn't never a-one on account of me.

My boss, he say they don't make drivers like me no more. Say I be the only one he can count on to show up on time and bring my bus in on time, never mind there be floods, detours, riots and all like that goin' on.

Ain't gonna be doin' it much longer though. No, sir. Just what's left of today and I'm done. Tonight when I brings this old bus in, I'll punch out, hand in my keys, tell the boss thanks for everythin' and go home. Retirin's what I'll be doin'. And none too soon.

Like I said, days seem awful long to me now. Time I goes to stand up and get off my bus at the end of my shift, these old legs of mine be so stiff it takes them awhile to start actin' like legs again and get me home.

And that ain't the whole of it. Legs ain't the only thing goin' on me. Mind's goin', too. There's times I get back to the depot nights and blessed if I can remember ever startin' out. Knows I sat behind the wheel all day. Din't have no accidents. Run no red lights. What I don't know is, who was drivin' while my mind was away someplace else? Only thing I can figure is I got a angel looking out for me.

Still and all, it ain't right. A body gettin' on a city bus has got to know the driver be payin' attention to what's goin' on right there and not what went on fifty years back in that little bitty town I come from to where I can still smell my Momma's cookin'… the chalk in that old schoolroom… warm chicken mash… And that's how come I told the boss man a month gone by I was fixin' to quit.

"You can't up and leave me, Clive," he says. "You're The Man. How'm I supposed to keep this place goin', train the new guys, if I don't have you to point at, say, 'Go ask Clive,' when they come askin' me to figure out their whole entire lives for 'em?"

Didn't tell him nothin' about my mind wanderin'. Just told him I was plain wore out. Said, "Time now for me to collect my pension, go set on a front porch someplace nice and quiet."

"Alright, Clive," he sighs. "Lord knows you earned it working like you done all these years, but... I'm gonna miss you somethin' fierce."

He turns to walk away, turns back. "Clive," he says, "I got one last favor to ask. You want to quit end of August, ain't that right?"

I said that was right.

"How's about," he goes, "you take me through the Labor Day week? Got a guy I'm trainin' now and if you could see your way to givin' me them few extra days he'll be all set to roll."

Said I'd do it. Heck, wasn't but a few more days. Glad now I did. Got to see my reg'lars another time or two and with the kids back in school since Tuesday, got to see little Miss Margaret again. My, but she growed over the summer!

Margaret's been ridin' with me goin' on three years now. Used to be her Momma brung her to the bus every day. "Take care of her for me, Clive," she'd call of a morning while Margaret climbed up the steps on them chubby little legs of hers. And, "Thank you, Clive," she'd say when I dropped her back off.

"Yes, ma'am," I'd call back, both goin' and comin', always suspectin' Miss Margaret was a mite bit discomfited with all that attention. Sure enough, last spring her Momma started lettin' her wait on the bus her own self.

An' there she be now, waitin' on me to take her home and I can't keep from smilin' just at the sight of her.

"It go good for you today, Miss Margaret?" I asks watchin' her climb on board on legs that went from chubby to skinny over the summer.

She gives me her bit of a smile, nods her head, and I gives her a wink, knowin' she ain't never been one to talk much. And then, like always, I watch in my rearview makin' sure she's found herself a seat and is settin' in it before I takes off.

I see there ain't but the one seat empty today and with her backpack darn near big as she is, Miss Margaret's takin' a minute figurin' which way to turn herself before settin' in it. Then I see the young fella that got on a while back holdin' out his hands to help with the backpack and Margaret, she ain't sure if that be OK or not. She makes up her mind and lets him take it while she settles herself and then he sets it on the floor and Margaret gives him her little smile.

I steers my bus through a couple busy intersections and next time I look I see the young fella and Miss Margaret is laughin' fit to bust and I'm surprised on account of Margaret don't gen'rally take to strangers.

Then I see how come they's laughin' and I smile myself seein' the young fella pull a quarter out his ear. Next thing I see, he's got one comin' out his mouth and Miss

Margaret's just tickled to death and I feel downright happy for her.

We're near about at the end of the line now and most of my passengers is gone—always has more gettin' off than on this time of day—and next time I look Mister Magician fumbles a quarter and it falls in Margaret's lap. The both of them grope for it and Margaret's a-wrigglin' and a-gigglin'.

He tries his trick a few more times and keeps on droppin' his quarter only... I see Margaret ain't laughin' no more. Fact is, she's lookin' downright confused and suddenly I get what's goin' on. That som'bitch be messin' with her!

I near about run into the back of a truck figurin' what am I gonna do about this here situation. Can't get the attention of them last few passengers, all of 'em settin' in back readin' their newspapers. Can't stop the bus go find a cop. Be the pervert's word against mine. 'Sides, might could be he's got a knife. A gun, maybe?

"Lord, help me," I prays, my heart beatin' louder'n a drum. "Show me the way."

Could keep the doors of the bus shut. Keep the creep from gettin' off with Margaret. Only then what? Can't drive around the whole entire night keepin' all my passengers prisoner and him doin' what he's doin'.

I'm about fifty feet from Margaret's stop now and I see she's standin' already, her face white and scared lookin', her eyes fixed fast to the floor. See the pervert

93

pull hisself up, too, reach for her backpack.

My hands be sweatin' so bad now I can't hardly hold the wheel steady and in my head I hear Margaret's Momma saying, "Take care of her for me, Clive."

Seems like that angel I got that takes over my drivin' once in a while be hearin' her, too, 'cause here we be, slowin' down. Pullin' in to the curb. Door's openin'.

Miss Margaret, she jumps down them steps like they's on fire and my heart near about quits seein' her run in front of the bus till I sees there ain't no traffic comin' either way and she's safe on the other side.

The pervert clears the steps, too, only Margaret's back pack twists in his hand, tangles with his legs, and he stumbles crossin' in front of the bus and goes down on his knees.

Right then my angel guy takes over again and lets up on the brakes just a bitty tad and the bus jolts the som'bitch all the way down. Not enough to hurt him, mind, just enough to scare him and keep him off balance and from following Miss Margaret. And I guess it worked 'cos she ain't nowhere to be seen.

And while I'm haulin' myself out my seat, stumblin' my way down the steps on legs I knows ain't never gonna walk right again, I see some folks has helped the pervert up on his feet and he's lookin' around like he don't know what happened. Like, he's askin' hisself how come he's gettin' all the attention when all he done was trip and fall and ain't one bit hurt.

As for me, I'm shakin' my head thinkin' I might could have lost my Safe Driver record. Maybe my pension? Don't make no never mind. I knows I done right by Miss Margaret and her Momma both, and I be satisfied.

I sees a cop that's been around near as long as me headin' over and I'm happy knowin' he'll take care the creep stays out this neighborhood when I gets done tellin' him what-all I seen. And when he's through writin' all that down, I'll tell him how just as soon's I'm done turning in my keys, I'm gonna stop back by Miss Margaret's house on my way home'n drop off her backpack so she won't be frettin' none over it.

I'll be done with all of it then and I can set myself down on my porch where it's real quiet and start in rockin' and praisin' the Lord for givin' me that angel. That angel that stuck with me clear the way through to the end of the line.

The Lonely Little Tree

A ll alone, in a vast meadow, grew a tree. It was a very young, very small tree, scarcely taller than the grasses that grew around it. And because it was alone, the only tree as far as the eye could see, it did not know the way of trees, nor even that it was a tree. All it knew was that it was. That, and the great, ever-changing sky above it with its shining sun and gleaming moon, its million stars and tumbling clouds. And all day, every day, the tree yearned towards that sky, thinking it a most beautiful and wondrous thing.

So intrigued, in fact, was the tree with the glory above it that for a very long time it was unaware of its own growth upwards or the silent spread of its roots growing deep and strong in the earth below. But one day, bending low beneath the worst storm in the memory of the meadow, the tree was astonished to discover that where before it had only one slender trunk, now, miraculously, branches grew in all directions from the thickened, sturdy trunk, and each branch was laden with the most beautiful leaves.

Right away the tree forgot all about the sky and the sun and the moon and the stars and turned all its attention to the magnificence of itself. And as it observed, it came to understand a most amazing and wonderful thing, which was that while each leaf was a part of the tree, it was "itself" too, unique, and unlike any of the other leaves, though all grew from the same source.

Another thing it came to understand was that each leaf had an entirely different view—and therefore, knowledge—of the meadow. One growing on an upper branch facing north, for example, would have little understanding of the small creatures and insects that scampered about in the undergrowth below. While a leaf on a lower limb, facing south, would know next to nothing about the many flocks of birds, and even bats, that sped by, or of changes in temperature and the direction of wind currents.

But because of them, the tree at their center knew all of their varying viewpoints and interests and each was as important and cherished by it as the next. For the tree loved all its leaves dearly, the way a parent loves its children, however different and varied their outlooks might be.

All through the soft days of spring and the hot days of summer, the tree gloried in its leaves and learned from them and basked in their loveliness.

But gradually, without the tree ever noticing, the days grew shorter and the sun lost its warmth. The tree didn't notice because it had more important things to think about. Namely, that all its leaves, which it had always known as green, were mysteriously turning into the most glorious shades of yellow and gold and scarlet and crimson, and the tree was bewitched by their beauty.

How wonderful, it thought, that of everything growing in this meadow, I am at the center of all this magnificence. And it was so happy it didn't notice that the wind, which it had always known as a gentle friend, was growing stronger and colder, until one day a terrible thing happened: one of its leaves, fluttering and dancing at the end of a limb, suddenly let go and without so much as a backward glance, floated away with the wind.

"Stop!" the tree cried out in dismay. "You can't just float away like that! Your place is here! You are a part of me! Why, without you I am less than I was. Come back!"

But even as it cried out, other leaves let go, too, and followed after the first and there was nothing the tree could do, nothing it could say, to make them stay.

Day after miserable day, as the wind grew colder and howled through its branches, the leaves continued to fly away, some in ones and twos, as though reluctant to part, others in great flurries, seeming eager to follow in the path of the wind, until there came a day, a terrible day, when the tree was without any leaves at all and stood alone and naked in the bitter cold.

"A fine friend you turned out to be," it called out in anguish to the wind. "Look what you've done to me!

You've taken away everything I loved and tossed them far and wide and now what's to become of me? Without my leaves to love and admire and learn from, I am nothing and I have nothing to do."

But the wind only laughed as it sped by. "Have patience, little tree," it called, "and rest while you can, for by-and-by, in the spring, I shall return softly and you will be surprised at how much everything will have changed."

But the tree, who was very young and had little memory of past winters or springs, didn't understand and cried out instead to the sky, the only other thing it had ever known. "I don't understand why this happened to me," it sobbed. "I really loved my leaves and I can't bear to be without them... It's too lonely... Can you tell me what to do or why I must stay here all alone?"

But the sky was dark and gray and tumbled by the wind itself and had no answer for the tree.

Then the tree had a wonderful idea and turned back eagerly to the wind. "I know just what to do!" it called. "Take me with you! Let me see where it is you go for surely it must be a wonderful place that everything hurries to join you on your journey."

"Some must go and some must stay," the wind roared. "You must stay, for that is the way of trees. And I must go because the way of the wind is to be forever in motion.

"On my travels I carry the rains and snows and seeds

and scatter them wherever they are needed, even to the far ends of the earth. Indeed, it was I who brought you here to this treeless meadow in the first place and it is I who has carried many of your seeds to other parts of this meadow and even further afield than that!"

"Very impressive, I'm sure," sneered the tree. "But really, it all seems rather pointless to me if in the end I'm to be left, lonely and ignorant, forever rooted in this boring place. What is the reason for my being here? What is my purpose?"

"This meadow is where you are supposed to be. Right here. Right now. And your purpose is the same as all the other species that live and grow upon the face of the earth: to be exactly who and what they are, which in your case, is a tree!" howled the wind. "That is all. To be yourself! To be happy! To be proud!"

"Of what?" the tree glowered. "For what?"

But the wind had no more time to spare and with a flourish disappeared behind a mountain top. And because now there was no sound, no movement in the frozen meadow, nothing to observe, nothing to listen to, the tree, in spite of itself, fell into the long sleep of winter.

The warmth and light of the sun awakened it. Not the pale, cold light of the winter sun, but the soft, warming glow of the spring sun.

The tree stirred and gazed about it and saw that the meadow, which it remembered as barren and frozen, was greening and that new life abounded everywhere.

"Thank you, little tree, for sheltering us this winter," said a mother rabbit, bringing her babies out of a burrow at the tree's base for their first warming rays of the sun. "Without your protection we certainly would have perished."

"Why... it was nothing," said the tree with a smile. "I was here anyway."

"Thank you for your delicious acorns that saved us from hunger all winter," said a sleepy little squirrel, yawning and stretching in the soft air.

"Well goodness gracious!" exclaimed the tree. "You mean those funny little things can be eaten?"

"Indeed, they can," said the squirrel. "Why, without them we could not live in this beautiful meadow at all. Surely you remember how busy we were at the end of summer gathering them up quickly before the cold wind would come to scatter them far and wide."

"Yes indeed, " the tree nodded. "I do remember. And that was very clever of you for it seems the wind sweeps everything before it. I'm glad you enjoyed them."

"Thank you for your strong branches," chirped a busy little robin. "In this nest I am building high above the ground, my young will be very safe."

"Oh... please make yourself at home," said the tree. "It's nice to know they can serve such a useful purpose."

Just then a gentle breeze came to hover above the

tree. "Now do you understand why you have to stay?" it whispered. "Do you see how necessary you are to the life of this meadow? And do you have any idea how much I will look forward to coming to rest amidst your cool green shade after a long journey across the rock-strewn mountains? Or the pleasure I will take in playing, however briefly, among your beautiful leaves before I continue my journey?"

"Oh, but you're mistaken," the tree said with a sigh. "Surely you remember that last autumn you came and took away all my leaves, scattering them here, there and everywhere. I'm afraid there are none left for you to play amongst."

The wind chuckled. "My young friend," it said. "You still have much to learn. Just look at yourself now! Why, you're a vision all decked out in your beautiful new leaves!"

"New leaves?" the tree gasped, drawing itself up tall. And sure enough, all of its branches were filled to bursting with bright, shiny new leaves.

"But…" the tree stammered. "I… I don't understand… Where did they come from?"

"They came from within you," the wind chuckled. "As does all new growth. And every spring for hundreds of years you will send out fresh leaves and every autumn I will come to take them away with me for it is in this way that the old always makes way for the new. And as you have now learned, when the winters come, as they always will, you will rest and gather your strength for your next crop of leaves and acorns. And meantime you will provide shelter for the small creatures that live here with you in this meadow."

"But… I still don't understand. What is the reason for all this?" the tree asked.

"It is for you to learn."

"To learn? To learn what?"

"The very special role you have to play in the grand life of the universe. To accept that change is necessary. To love and let go. To give of yourself. To understand that you are important, needed and loved. And this, my friend, is true whether you are covered in leaves or not."

"All that?" the tree exclaimed. "That is a lot to learn!"

"Yes, it is," the wind agreed. "But don't worry, every year it will get easier. And as you grow, so will your wisdom, until there will come a day when you become a fine example to others."

"Oh… I don't know about that," the tree faltered. "I don't think I'll ever be wise enough or special enough to set an example to others. I mean, come on… I'm only a tree."

"Only a tree, indeed!" the wind exploded. "Why, just as you once noticed that none of your leaves grew exactly like another, so I, endless traveler that I am, can tell you that while there are millions of trees growing upon the earth, some on mountains, some in deserts, some looking down on busy city streets, others on tropical beaches, nowhere, but nowhere in the world is there another tree just exactly like you."

"Nowhere!" exclaimed the tree. "Good heavens! That does make me feel rather special. In fact, it makes me feel quite unique. Perhaps then… I mean… just possibly, I could get used to the idea of setting an example to others after all. But what, indeed who, in the world could learn anything from me?"

"Sometimes you try my patience, little tree," the wind snapped. "Surely you must have noticed by now that everything learns from everything else! Think of what you learned from the sky, the clouds, the moon, the stars! And what about the animals? Think of all you learned from them!

"Now, think about all the tiny acorns I scattered last autumn that even now are pushing their way to the surface of this very meadow. To whom will they turn, if not to you, to learn of themselves?

Looking ahead even further, you must realize that through them your own learning will increase as you see yourself mirrored in them."

"This sounds like it could be fun!" said the little tree.

"It is! It is!" agreed the wind. "Why, life is the grandest adventure of all! And when you truly understand that every living thing, no matter the differences in appearance, customs, place of birth, way of life, is exactly where it's supposed to be, doing exactly what it's supposed to be doing, then you will have learned the most valuable lesson of all, little tree. "

"I will?" gasped the tree. "Quickly. Tell me what it is."

"You will have learned to love and accept yourself exactly the way you are!" said the wind. "And in doing so, that love will grow to include all other living things. and free you to accept them just exactly as they are.

"And that, little tree, is the greatest lesson of all and the reason you are here—to love!"

And with a sw-o-o-osh the wind went laughing away across the mountain top.

Peace of Mind

Martha is in a tizzy—has been for a few days, as a matter of fact—and understandably, she's not at all happy about it. After all, it's been a good ten years, since right after the death of her husband of thirty years and the marriage of her youngest child, that she set out to completely reinvent herself. And now here she is, falling apart, just like in the old days. Enough to make even a saint weep, is what she tells herself.

Knowing that old habits are notoriously hard to break, Martha had not taken on her reinvention process lightly. But she'd had a feeling that if she didn't make the effort then, when for the first time in her life she had the freedom and time to do exactly what *she* wanted, it would be too late. Besides, she'd felt confident that by getting both herself and her life organized and under control once and for all, she'd finally be able to enjoy what had evaded her all her life: peace of mind.

She'd set-to with a vengeance, her top priority being to sell the old, untidy, rambling house where all six of her children had grown up and buying a nice quiet, tidy little house where, at last, everything would have a place of its own and stay there until she, of her own accord and in her own time, was ready to move it somewhere else.

This accomplished, along with ridding herself of all the old beat-up furniture and the residue of bikes, skates, sleds, board games, dolls and assorted junk her kids had accumulated, then left behind, she'd turned her attention to herself.

Exercising and losing weight had, of course, been at the top of her list, followed closely by mastering the art of applying make up correctly, a skill she acquired over a matter of weeks at various beauty counters at various Malls.

Next, she traded her glasses for contacts, made herself a whole new wardrobe, and got rid of her white hair by having it colored a becoming shade of ash brown with just a few, subtly placed, blonde highlights. She'd even surprised herself, whilst sitting in the beauty salon waiting for the color to take, to throw in a manicure—her first ever—for good measure. In for a penny, in for a pound, was what she told herself.

As you can imagine, the difference between the old Martha and the new was almost shocking. She'd given herself a good twenty years in appearance and her kids were starting to worry about what might come next. An extravagant shopping spree? A boy friend? Maybe even a new husband? Gasp! Or what if she attempted an around-the-world cruise? After all, this new mother of theirs positively sparkled and while they applauded all her efforts, their main concern had become, when will it all end?

Not soon.

For Martha had not just set out to change her appearance—no silly little airhead was she—but also included becoming ruthless with herself in making, and sticking to, a schedule so that never again would she be lost in the indecision and self-doubt that had plagued her all her life. She'd had quite enough of that, thank you. Going forward she intended to make every minute of every day count. There were to be no more half-finished projects, abandoned classes, or mislaid items cluttering up her home or her life.

Finally, to complete her metamorphosis—and even though she quaked inwardly—Martha squared her shoulders and went out to find herself a job. Not just any old job, mind you, but one where her newly created persona could continue to flourish, not only for her own benefit, but for those for whom she worked.

After an exhaustive search, she chose to become the receptionist at the oldest, most prestigious law firm in the city.

Interviewing for this job, she'd smiled and nodded in vigorous agreement when the head of human resources stressed the importance of both appearance and work habits in that particular position, saying, "Since the receptionist is the first person our clients, prospective clients and visitors see on entering our offices, it is vital that the one we choose be meticulously organized and appropriately dressed at all times."

Martha had more than lived up to expectations. "Marvelous Martha," was how she came to be known by the entire staff when they spoke of her serene and ever-present smile, the way she had taken it upon herself to be the first member of the staff to arrive each morning, allowing plenty of time to make sure the reception area was pristine, the coffee made, and, in all seasons, some fresh little flowers, or sprigs of evergreen from her garden, on the corner of her desk.

Drawing upon her long-standing dressmaking skills—she had, after all, sewn for her three girls, birth through marriage, including, even, their wedding gowns—Martha made a point of showing up for work each day with some charming little touch—a pin, a scarf, a flower—added to whatever outfit she was wearing that had all the female staffers shaking their heads and asking how in the world she dreamed them up.

It goes without saying that Martha was a whiz on the phones, managing somehow or other to field all incoming calls by at least the third ring, and keeping those "on hold" from losing patience and hanging up.

And nobody could fail to notice that in times of stress when various law partners were throwing both tantrums and files and the rest of the staff were scurrying around like frightened rabbits, Martha and her reception area remained the calm at the center of the storm.

When other staff members asked her secret, Martha smiled her beautiful smile and said, "It's all about staying organized, darlings. Just make yourself a schedule and stick to it no matter what. Try it. You'll see."

She smiled because experience had taught her that no matter how often she repeated this, there wasn't a single one among those who asked who would do a thing about taking her advice seriously, thinking it far too simple a solution for the rampant chaos in their own lives.

The fact is, though, that getting organized had been the toughest nut Martha had had to crack in her reinvention process, coming as she did from a background that had never, ever included herself or what she wanted but centered, rather, on her husband and the kids with their endless extra-curricular activities, their pets, their friends, their health, their ambitions, their athletics, their homework. A life in which her chief role had been that of chauffeur and cook and where one hectic day seeped into the next with never a moment to stop and draw breath. And one in which, at each day's end, she took to her bed with the dissatisfied feeling that nothing noteworthy had been accomplished nor satisfactorily completed.

The new Martha, therefore, had been ruthless with herself in allowing no distractions until she mastered the art of organization, not just on the job, but in every facet of her life.

What she did was become a miser of minutes. In Martha's life, there was now no wasted time thus ensuring her the peace and quiet she craved and the leisure to enjoy every second. For example, Martha would never waste her precious time on a weekend running errands. That would not be efficient. Errands, she would tell you, are something you do on your way to and from work.

"Why make a special project," she'd ask, "of going out to do one silly little errand when it can be done either coming or going?"

Martha isn't one to brag, but one of the first things she did after acquiring her job, was switch her bank account and dry cleaners from the branches in the suburbs she'd used for decades, to those within walking distance of her office. In this way, she advised, such errands could be accomplished in the lunch hour, on foot, thus saving not only time but money.

When people asked for clarification on this point, she'd have to bite her tongue not to scream at their lack of imagination before saying, "You get in your exercise and you save on gas!" Biting her tongue not to add, "Duh!"

You will never find Martha wasting time on the weekend doing household chores either. No, no and no! Her weekends are for sleeping late, taking naps, enjoying the Sunday paper, watching TV, reading, working in her little garden and visiting her children and numerous grandchildren, all of it done with the blissful knowledge that every facet of her carefully structured life was in perfect order.

Early on in her reinvention process she had discouraged the children—very tactfully, of course—from visiting her because, since moving to the smaller house, she simply didn't have room for them all. Besides, with her tight schedule and high-stress job there was simply no time for the massive preparation and clean-up required for any of their visits. In the order of their birth, then, it was she who visited them, one family at a time, on succeeding Saturday afternoons

All household chores were now scheduled for the evenings, usually immediately upon her return from the office when she was still in what she called, "high gear."

It should be noted here that even if Martha had to work overtime, which was often the case, she would not rest until those evening chores were completed though they may keep her up till well after eleven. This, she insisted, was the only way, to keep things from piling up.

Mondays evenings, then, were for laundry. Tuesdays for ironing, mending and working on new outfits. Wednesdays for turning the cushions on the couches and easy chairs in her living room as well as cleaning mirrors and her few pieces of silver. Thursdays were for dusting, where she paid particular attention to the framed photographs of her late husband, the six children and all the grandchildren. She would have been reluctant to admit it, but she found it so much easier to love and appreciate them, silent and smiling at her from under glass in their sparkling frames, than she had when they were all rampaging through her house creating chaos, demanding attention, and driving her to distraction.

By the way, Thursdays were also for the bathrooms.

And Fridays? Well Fridays, were something else. Fridays, Martha left the house ten minutes earlier than usual in order to fill her gas tank and squeegee her windshield. For some reason the squeegee at the gas station always seemed to work better than the one she had at home. And on her way home she stopped at her local supermarket to replenish the groceries and sundry other items that had found their way to her list over the week.

And still Friday was not over for Martha. Once home she still had to put her groceries away, eat her evening meal—she always treated herself to a frozen dinner with ice cream for dessert on Fridays—and then set about vacuuming the whole house, top to bottom and front to back.

Now, of course, Martha would be the first to concede that a schedule such as hers was not for everybody. It was certainly demanding. But the charm of it all was that if, say, she noticed the laundry piling up on a Wednesday, or dust gathering on a Monday, she wouldn't drop what she was doing at the time and deal with them as she had in the old days. No more of that, thank you. Now she would simply recognize that Monday was the day for laundry, Thursday the day for dusting, and go on happily with what she was doing.

Oh, the freedom that knowledge gave her. The blissful peace of mind. To put it simply then, Martha's system worked like a charm for her. Or it did, until a recent Friday...

That Friday, right on schedule, Martha was just finishing breakfast, when a single line in the newspaper caught her eye. Her whole body went rigid. She gasped, blinked, looked again. To get a grip on herself and still her fast-beating heart, she allowed herself a minute to look out the kitchen window where she could see the early morning sun just peeking through the leaves of her sturdy oak, before looking back at the paper. Then, as was her habit, she glanced at the clock and saw she was a couple of minutes behind schedule. Scrambling to her feet, she unplugged the coffee maker, put her dirty dishes in the dishwasher, applied lipstick, double checked that all appliances were on OFF, and headed for the Mobil station.

But she was preoccupied, Martha, and not at all her usual, serene, smiling self. A small frown creased her brow most of the day to be intercepted now and then by a dazed, almost vacant look. The people in her office noticed the change in her demeanor at once and muttered about it among themselves.

"What's with Martha?" they asked one another hearing the phones ringing non-stop. The briefs she had been asked to copy lying every which way by the machine. The files and memos cluttering her desk.

What was with Martha was that she had a battle raging inside her head wherein that line in the newspaper, with all its possible ramifications, threatened to take precedence over the smiling tranquility she'd come to expect of herself. Enough to drive a sane person crazy was how she attempted to reassure herself.

All day the battle raged as she struggled to stay organized and on schedule and Martha was mortified. She hated it. Never in her life had she felt so completely frazzled and incompetent. Not even when the kids were little and all six came down with chicken pox the very same day that the dog ran away and the water pipes in the cellar burst.

By the end of it—the day, that is—Martha was worn out and near tears. All she wanted was to go home and go to bed. But how could she? She had to get the mess on her desk straightened out no matter how long it took. And she still had to stop for groceries, put them away, eat, vacuum...

"Hope you feel better soon," various staff members called out as they passed her desk at the end of the day.

"Yeah," said others, "go home and treat yourself to a nice long rest. You look beat."

Easy for them, Martha thought with a scowl. Easy for them...

Pulling into her driveway that evening, way later than usual, Martha hit the automatic garage door opener, eased her car into the garage, turned off the motor, then sat slumped in her seat behind the wheel and tried to put the whole awful day behind her before she tackled what lay ahead. Then she brightened. Heck, she had the whole weekend in front of her. She'd deal with it all tomorrow. Tonight she'd just do her vacuuming, enjoy her frozen dinner and ice cream, and put her feet up.

Then she remembered this was the last Friday of the month. That meant hair-coloring night. Darn. She'd have to do it though. She'd noticed gray showing at her temples a couple of days ago. Oh, well... So she'd stay on schedule... vacuum... color her hair... get some sleep... and tomorrow... Why, tomorrow she'd make up a whole new schedule taking into account the line in the paper and everything would fall into place as it always did.

Immediately she started to feel better and smiled to herself. Nobody knew better than she that everything always became manageable once you found a place for it on a schedule. Too bad she hadn't taken a moment to think of that this morning. Could've saved herself a really messy day. She shuddered anew thinking of how she'd behaved. No wonder everyone had been looking at her sideways. God, she'd really lost it. She shrugged, consoling herself that any one of them would have lost it, too, if they'd seen what she'd seen and it applied to them.

Surprisingly, Martha slept well that night, enjoyed her usual Saturday morning sleep-in and extra special breakfast that always included Danish and a second cup of coffee, and it wasn't until she was finishing up that her brain started short-circuiting again as she pondered the best way to proceed.

Of course, she'd get her gardening out of the way first else it would be bugging her all day. The roses desperately needed cutting back and the whole yard was ready for its mid-summer fertilizing. That done she could mulch the beds, get the sprinklers going and then... dive in.

Check the newspaper first, she decided, make sure her eyesight hadn't failed her. Then call the kids. As always, she'd start with the eldest and go on down the list. Of course, there would be those who would want to call an emergency meeting right away, especially the middle two who always had more to say than she cared to listen to. And there would be others who, uninvited, would throw their kids in the car and come right over filled with advice and warnings, insisting that she get second opinions and consult with experts.

She knew she couldn't deal with any of it. No way. Not today. She had the whole bunch landing on her doorstep, they'd start arguing amongst themselves and she'd have a zoo going on with the whole day wasted listening to them, waiting on them, cleaning up after them. No! Forget the kids. She'd handle it on her own. At least for the time being.

What then? Make other calls, she supposed. She wasn't sure yet who to, but there would have to be other calls. Maybe the newspaper would be a good place to start? Ask if they were sure of their facts. After all, newspapers make mistakes just like everybody else. Otherwise they wouldn't always be printing retractions along with apologies, would they? Then, if it was correct, she'd ask if they knew of a specialist in the field who could steer her in the right direction? Come to think of it, she couldn't be the only one who had ever found themselves in such a situation. And if they didn't know, well...she'd have to come up with something on her own.

Meanwhile, the gardening wasn't going too well. Once outside, Martha forgot what it was she'd planned and found herself cutting back the azaleas instead of the roses and everybody knows you don't cut back azaleas mid-summer. She looked around blankly trying to remember what it was that needed pruning. Everything looked OK to her. Had to be something though. She should have made a list is what she should have done, darn it. She knew better.

Really, this was getting ridiculous. She was beginning to act the way she had yesterday and it simply wasn't good enough. Just like coloring her hair last night. She'd forgotten to set the timer and had no idea when to rinse the coloring solution out of her hair. She'd studied herself carefully in the mirror and darned if she could tell if it looked under or over. In the end she'd opted for over and rinsed it out thinking it wasn't worth risking losing her entire head of hair over an oversight. But once she blow-dried it she'd seen that she must have been under because the gray was still showing at the temples. Really, the amount of time wasted! Enough to drive a sane person crazy.

She was about to give up on her yard when she remembered the mulch. Good! That had definitely been on her non-existent list. That meant she was thinking straight again, thank God. She was half way through when she suddenly remembered she hadn't fertilized yet. She always fertilized before mulching. Biting her lip with frustration, she got the bag of fertilizer out of the garage, hauled it round back and began spreading it around the bushes. But wait a minute. Didn't she always do the grass first so if she ran short she wouldn't have half a bright green lawn and half a yellowing one? Of course she did.

At a trot she headed for the garage to get the spreader, tripped over a protruding root at the base of the oak, twisted her ankle, and fell to her knees howling with pain and frustration. Now what was she supposed to do? Couldn't go on working on a foot that was already swelling, could she? Couldn't leave the gardening tools she'd already used spread out all over the yard like a garage sale was in progress, could she?

Picking up the garden rake, using it as a crutch, wincing with pain at every step, she gathered up the scattered tools and threw them in the garage, made her way up the back steps and into the kitchen where, still using the rake as a crutch, she got ice out of the freezer, filled a large bowl with it, added water, put her injured foot in it and tried to think what needed to be done next. Wasn't she supposed to visit one of the kids today? Of course she was. It was Saturday, wasn't it?

Only... which one? She couldn't remember! And her foot hurt too much to go check her calendar. Besides, she hadn't thought to get a towel out prior to plunging her foot in the water and if she took it out now she'd have puddles all over the floor and could slip and fall. She'd just have to wait and let the foot air-dry, that's all.

More time wasted.

Poor Martha! All through that day and the next, she struggled—fought—to be the person she'd trained herself to be: a serene, unflappable woman in total control of herself and every moment of her day. And the more she worked at it, the more difficult it became and it seemed incomprehensible to her that the hard won habits of the past decade could have been so totally disrupted by one stray line in a newspaper.

By the end of it—that is by Sunday evening—she was on the verge of hysterics. Her house, her yard, and herself were a shambles. Half finished lists and schedules littered every room in the house. She hadn't showered or brushed her teeth. Hadn't even changed clothes. Hadn't put anything away including the spreader outside and the bowl of water inside. Hadn't eaten anything sensible. Hadn't washed a single dish. And she'd been hyper-ventilating and in tears since lunchtime, knowing, without a shadow of a doubt, that she could not go to the office tomorrow and function at all, never mind at anything like her usual level. Particularly not since, somewhere along the way, she remembered she'd forgotten her usual stop for gas on Friday morning and her car was on empty.

And then, out of nowhere, a stray thought crossed her mind. A thought that changed everything: Forget you ever saw it.

She frowned, sat up straighter. Forget you ever saw it?

But... ?

Yet even as she questioned those words and what they implied, she felt the tension drain out of her. Her head came up, her shoulders went back, she dried her tears, she even smiled.

Of course! That's all she had to do. Forget she ever saw it. Not only was it the best and simplest solution, it was the only solution for nothing was worth living as she had these past few days. Nothing.

On a deep breath, she stood up and hobbling,

clutching and leaning against various tables and chairs, she made her way to Friday's paper, which still lay where she had let it fall. From there she moved to her purse, lying where she had tossed it on her return from work, and pulled out her wallet. Groping in the back pocket where she kept her most important slips of paper and her emergency hundred dollar bill, she clawed out her lottery ticket with her index finger and compared the numbers to the ones in the paper. Yep. Just as she suspected. They matched. With a satisfied nod and maybe just the tiniest twinge of regret, she jammed the offending page of the paper into the shredder—always kept handy under the kitchen table—and smiled as it noisily did its job.

Now for the ticket. She was tempted to put it in the shredder, too, but thought better of it feeling it only right that she shred it with her own two hands. Carefully then, with great concentration, she tore it in half, then in half again, and again, and again until she had a sizable pile of tiny little specs of paper before her.

Then, to be quite sure she would never, ever lay eyes on them again, or give them a second thought, she brushed the pieces into the sink and, lighting a match, watched them turn into charred ashes. Giggling now, blowing them a light-hearted farewell kiss, she flushed them into the drain and turned on the garbage disposal. There! It was over.

She could forget she ever saw it.

Sure... Seven and a half million dollars would have been nice. But she wasn't stupid, Martha, and she'd learned something over the past few days, something very valuable: all the dollars in the world could not buy back her most prized possession, her hard-won peace of mind.

(Good thing she never told the kids, huh?)

Battle Fatigue

I've been an angel since as far back as I can remember—read forever—so, obviously, I'm a bit of an expert on how things are run over here.

The same can be said of my knowledge of what goes on over on your side. And one of the conclusions I've reached is that most of you mortals think of angels as musically gifted beings of light who float around the Universe dispensing comfort and assistance to anyone who needs them, 24/7. And you're right. There are those among us who do just that. It's their pride, pleasure and privilege to "know" when they're needed and to be there for you.

But there are also those among us who reside permanently on your side and there are several things about them I bet you didn't know, which may come as a bit of a surprise. For example, once in a very great while these particular angels get to feeling a bit overwhelmed by the sheer immensity of their task. I guess what I'm really saying here is that, believe it or not, they get tired. I've experienced it myself and seen it in others.

Now don't get me wrong. When I say tired, I'm not speaking of the kind of bone-weary fatigue you mortals experience when you've been on the job too long, or the kids are taking their sweet time growing up, or you've pushed yourself too far in some kind of sport. That kind of fatigue can usually be remedied by a good long sleep or a nice vacation.

And keep in mind that every so often you mortals get to go "on break." By which I mean you get to go to heaven for as long as you please—centuries, if you feel like it—before starting over in a whole new life.

It's different for us angels. As most of you know we're eternal beings, which means we can expect to be "on the job" forever. Now that might sound a bit daunting, but remember, we don't have the same concept of "time" as you. No. Angels have their being in the eternal "present." Or, to put it another way, we are always in the "Now." So there's the difference. I guess you could say then that what we suffer from is more like an occasional bout of battle fatigue rather than "tired" as you understand it.

In other words, it's as if we're the Red Cross to the entire Universe on a permanent basis. And that's as it should be. We know how important it is for humans to feel that we're there for them and, rest assured, we are and always will be.

Obviously, Strategic Planning is very much in place with us. Has to be. Think of the chaos if every angel had to be on alert for every human in every corner of the earth. Wouldn't work, would it?

Therefore, our Planners allot each of us a specific

geographical section of the planet and keep close tabs that we stick to our given territory. "Straying" is frowned upon.

To be sure, there are times when we get the "All hands on deck" call. You should have seen us at the time of the Great Flood! But as you know events like that are rare and, generally speaking, we are able to stay in our assigned neighborhoods.

Another thing you might not know is that one of our biggest perks—indeed, the one that keeps us happily moving forward, ad infinitum—is job satisfaction.

There's nothing quite like the feeling we get when we've helped a mortal through some predicament that seemed hopeless and then get to watch them shaking their heads and wondering ever after just what happened.

Makes us feel special that, and that's the beauty of angel work—and the fun—our subtlety; our ability not to leave so much as a trace, no, not even a hint, of our divine intervention.

We have a lot of fun with it in our few slow times, comparing notes and showing each other videos of just where and when we stepped in to provide the magic. By that I mean, those chance encounters that weren't chance at all. The wrong turns we engineer. The overheard remarks that are, in fact, carefully rehearsed. The so-called accidents, coincidences and the new one they're all talking about, the serendipities. I swear, some of us are so good we can even keep each other baffled for eons.

Job diversity is another thing that keeps us happily intrigued. Doesn't matter how long we've all been doing this—try forever—you humans are always coming up with some new situation to confound us until we figure out how best to intervene and, generally speaking, we have to be pretty quick about it. Most times when we're needed, it's RIGHT NOW. Think fires, explosions, tornadoes, a lunatic at a mall with a hatchet and you'll get my drift.

Did you know angels are not allowed to have favorites? Nope. In our line of work, it's strictly forbidden. Like it or not, we're here for everybody. But I will admit we have a soft spot for those who don't take credit themselves for some deftly averted disaster but readily admit there had to have been outside help.

"Somebody up there must really love me," they'll say. Or, "My angel must have been working overtime today to get me out of that one, boy!"

We're also aware that what might seem a mere bump in the road to one mortal, may be the end of the world to another—I use the term loosely—and it is not up to us to judge. If we pick up even the merest hint of distress from one of our allotted flock then it behooves us to tune in and do everything in our power to straighten it out.

Sometimes this might take minutes, other times days or even weeks. But again, remember that time, as such, only applies to your side of the equation, and we regret any seeming lapse or inconvenience this causes you. If you could, at such times, practice a little patience, it would be a great help.

I've got a call coming in right now and I recognize it as from one I've helped a time or two in the past. Fortunately, she is one of those I just mentioned who give credit, shall we say, to those outside themselves, which inclines me not to put her "on hold" for even so much as a half of one of your seconds.

I say this because I just this instant wrapped up a lengthy intervention between feuding family members who were all set to kill one another over an inheritance, preceded by a tsunami of gigantic proportions and I'd really been looking forward to taking a moment to kick back and regroup, so to speak.

Now, when I said I was picking up a distress signal, I didn't mean that it was someone calling out for me by name. Great heavens, how presumptuous would that be? I'm not God, am I? Besides, if that were the case then I would have failed miserably at my job which is to remain, in true angel fashion, totally invisible and totally anonymous.

No, this is simply a mortal who is in a great state of stress at the moment. "Freaking out," is how she puts it, and who is looking around for ways to get herself through what lies ahead.

Focusing, I see that she has just returned home after

an exceedingly trying day on the job. (I've been meaning to work on a way of getting her out of that job, but got sidetracked by the feuding family. It's on my list though and I'll get to it first chance I get.)

Right now, she is in tears and she's hyper-ventilating. She is getting ready to go out. She is running late. Her make-up and hair are a mess. She's so distraught she can't even decide what to wear. I cause a nice little suit to slide off its hanger knowing it's a "go anywhere" kind of outfit. She starts to kick it aside, changes her mind, grabs it up and pulls it on.

We're making progress.

Seems she's on her way to attend her youngest child's high school graduation ceremony. That's odd. Nothing to get upset about, if you ask me. But there again, it's not my place to judge. I will say, though, that the high school graduations of her other children were always joyful events in which she, as a single mom, took great pride. What's different?

Oh... I get it. Apparently she has to attend this one alone whereas in the past she's been surrounded by family and friends. She's upset more for her son than for herself, or so she says.

How's he going to feel, she wonders, looking around the auditorium for his cheering committee and finding just her—all by herself—while all his classmates will have both parents, both sets of grandparents, the aunts, the uncles, the siblings, the friends cheering them on?

Silly Jane! For someone who has been through some very traumatic, highly disturbing experiences, I must say she really is making a mountain out of this particular molehill. I know that boy of hers well and I can tell you for a fact he couldn't care less. He's not the kind who would even notice.

But there you are. She's distraught. Feels she's a failure as a mom even though she knows she did everything in her power to have a reunion type thing going on.

The boy's siblings are all unavoidably out of town—two of them overseas—and both sets of grandparents live out of state and have given up driving. The aunts and uncles? There are none. The friends? All legitimately busy. But that's not good enough for Jane. She feels she should have done more. Could have done more...

What's an angel to do? In spite of all my powers I can't materialize people, can I?

No, but I can be a "people." Just for a short time anyway, and show up for her. Actually, I quite enjoy taking on a human stance once in a while. It's interesting. It's fun. It's a change. It's what I meant earlier when I talked about job diversification.

Still in tears, she's in her car heading for the school now and I've alerted a few of my "traffic" buddies to see she doesn't wreck on the way. They'll see she gets green lights when she needs them, red when something up ahead looks dicey; put a steadying hand on the speed freaks out there, divert the cops, find her a parking space.

Me, I'm in the auditorium waiting for her to walk in so I can steer her to a seat—without her knowing I'm there, of course—with a spare beside it for me.

My, but she really is running late. But not a problem. I created a small diversion behind the scenes to delay the ceremony by ten minutes.

Ah, here she comes now. She's standing frozen in the doorway appalled by the number of people present and wondering where she's going to find a seat. The setting sun can be seen through the windows and by adjusting a ray of it, which causes it to flicker, I direct her gaze up to the balcony and she sees the seats I've chosen and I know what she's thinking—apart, that is, from wishing she could just turn tail and run.

She's thinking, I'm the only person standing... Everybody's staring at me... Where am I going to sit...? The only available seats are way up there in the balcony immediately overlooking the stage... That means I'm going to be seen by everybody in the entire auditorium and I'll have to disturb everybody in that long row to get to it... Why did I wear high heels? I sound like a member of the Gestapo clomping up these old wood stairs and along the aisles and everybody, just everybody, is staring at me. A woman alone? Gasp! Whoever heard of such a thing? At a graduation ceremony? Oh, God, I feel so stupid! So ugly... So useless...

I watch her fumble her way past all the seated people in the row and, sure enough, every eye in the place is on her. Some in the row stand to let her pass, others just move their knees sideways. She's muttering apologies... mopping her sweaty forehead... babbling... trying to smile... stay calm...

I wait till she's finally seated and then, to distract her, I do what she just did: disturb a good thirty people making my way to the seat next to hers. The last seat in the row.

She watches me approach and, again, I know what she's thinking...

She's thinking, I hope this old fart isn't going to sit next to me. He can't. I couldn't stand it. He might want to talk. Ask questions. And I'm not up for it. Anyway, why would he choose to sit way up here of all places? He can't be here alone. Nobody goes to a ceremony like this alone. A man like that has got to belong to some family group. Somebody's grandfather, maybe? An uncle? Oh, what I wouldn't give to tell him I'm holding this one empty seat for someone... A friend, maybe... If I had one...

Actually, I'm quite pleased with my "disguise".

I'm wearing an old tweed suit—with appropriate shirt and tie, of course—glasses, and a beard. I'm chubby. Mostly bald, but white-haired where I'm not. And I look exactly like somebody's grandfather, except, like her, I'm alone.

I get myself comfortable and wait a beat or two to let her get used to my being there and then I start with the small talk.

"I'm late. It's been a while since I got caught up in traffic like what's going on out there right now. Lord! Couldn't find a place to park. Crowded in here, too, huh? Not an empty seat in the place. Lord, is it hot in here, or is it just me? Wish they'd start these things a little later. You here for a son or a daughter? Oh, me too. Only for me it's a grandson.

I sense her relaxing.

"Yes," I tell her in answer to her question. "The family is here," and I wave my arm in a vague sort of way taking in the whole auditorium. "Somewhere... Then again, maybe not... Could be they're stuck in traffic, too."

And now the graduates are streaming in and everyone in the place is craning for a view of "their" precious loved one, her included.

"Point him out to me, your son," I say, knowing ahead of time she's not going to be happy when she sets eyes on him and she'll need someone to talk her through it. She nods, still craning.

I hear her gasp then, just like I knew she would. See her bury her face in her hands. She's horrified. Wants to die right there.

Every one of the graduates are wearing dark red robes, except one. Her son. His is fire-engine red.

"How can that be?" she sobs. "My other sons wore

it and they matched up with everybody else. Unless...
Unless the school sent out a memo that the little creep
never delivered?"

"You know what," I say. "I bet that's what happened.
He forgot to give it to you. But I like the way he looks.
The robe distinguishes him. Sets him apart from the
crowd. And you can see he's loving it. Look at the grin
he's wearing. The spotlight is all on him."

She lowers her hands, takes another look. "You think
so?" she murmurs. "Really?"

I nod vigorously. She smiles, her shoulders straighten.
"You're right," she says. "He does look good. And he
always wants to be different. Loves it, in fact. Maybe he
did it on purpose?"

"Could be," I say. "Could be." And now she's
pretty much back to normal. She's breathing evenly,
remembering her manners.

"And your grandson?" she begins. "Point him out to me."

I make another vague sort of gesture in the direction of
the graduates. "He's there somewhere," I say. "Blessed
if I know where, though. Fact is, I haven't seen him in a
couple of years. Don't know if I'd even recognize him."

She joins me in a chuckle and the conversation turns
to other things. Where am I visiting from? (If she only
knew!) How long will I be staying? How many children/
grand children do I have? More vague talk of other
ceremonies in other places.

We stand and clap as the ceremony comes to an end

and begin to make our way out of the auditorium. She turns to say she enjoyed meeting me. Hopes I find my family, my grandson, in the mob.

We start to descend the stairs to the lower floor and she turns to say something else, but... I'm already three states away in response to a call that just came in. A guy in a subway with a machine gun. Do you wonder why I say it's like we're the Red Cross? But, knowing my work with her was done, that her equanimity was restored, I left feeling very satisfied.

As for her, frowning, baffled, she's staring at the empty space I had occupied right behind her. She scans the shuffling crowd, looks up behind her, looks in the stairwell below, stands on tiptoe the better to see... cranes her neck... wonders where the heck I got to? How I could of just sort of... disappeared?

She thinks of me every so often. Still wonders who that kindly old soul was and if he caught up with his family. Even relates the incident to her friends wanting to know what they make of it.

The part I enjoy the most is when she gets to the end and tells how I just vanished. "Like... like as if he vaporized without a trace!" she gasps. "On a narrow flight of stairs?"

And the friends, as baffled as she is, shake their heads, spread their hands, shrug.

Oh, yes! The old job satisfaction! I certainly savored it that night.

A Long Ago Christmas

It should have been the worst Christmas imaginable and, to the adults of that time, I'm sure it was. But I was just five years old then, my brother Charles, six, and to us it was magical.

It was the first Christmas of the war and the dreaded Mr. Hitler, as Charles and I called him, had disrupted our peaceful, well-ordered, English-village lives as only a mad man could.

"One would think the chap lived in the village, the trouble the blighter is putting us to," my father complained in the midst of digging a room-sized hole in the back garden and covering it first with corrugated metal and then sand bags. The interior of this pit was also lined with sandbags and steps, of a sort, were hewn out of the earth and reinforced with old lumber.

Every garden in our village had one of these air raid shelters and at first they were a great novelty to the children, but soon rain had them all inches deep in water and when the air raid sirens went off, it was misery to grovel in them listening to the drone of enemy bombers and the dreaded thuds of falling bombs. Still, it took courage to come out when the "all clear" sounded for who knew what had been hit, maybe even destroyed.

"The bastards," the grown-ups would mutter, shaking their heads at smoking ruins and, although Charles and I were strictly forbidden to swear, everyone seemed strangely deaf when we, too, referred to the enemy as "the bastards."

It was "the bastards" fault that coal, our only source of heat, was practically non-existent; that the bathtub had a black ring painted in it at the three inch line to save water; that all the curtains in the house had been dyed black.

It was "their" fault too that our mother was driven to near distraction trying to stretch food when our once bountiful table was reduced to meager, rationed supplies, powdered milk and bread the color of cement.

"Lord help the Londoners," she would say as we tended our victory garden. "At least we can grow a few vegetables out here in the country."

We grew more than a few. "Seems to me I'm digging my way through this bloody war," Daddy grumbled as he turned over yet another patch of his prized lawn to more rows of everything.

In the same way we lost all our flower beds to rhubarb, black currants, raspberries and strawberries, nasty, mean-tempered chickens soon moved into my favorite place in the world: a dear little summer house in the prettiest part of the garden.

Because of "the bastards" every inhabitant of our

village was issued with gas masks and although my mother made light of them and sewed brightly colored, waterproof shoulder bags to carry them in, they were an ugly reminder of what the mad Hitler might come up with next.

"Why do we have to wear these beastly things?" I spluttered, trying mine on for the first time. "They smell awful! Ugh! Rubbery. And they pinch my face and the strap gets tangled in my hair. I hate it! It hurts! I won't wear it!"

"But, darling," consoled my mother. "Think how frightened a German would be if he crashed nearby and saw us all with these funny rubber masks on. He'd run away he'd be so frightened. Besides, Mr. Churchill wants you to wear them."

"But…"

"And so do the King and Queen."

They went with us everywhere, those masks. To school, to church, to the shops and, of course, to the air raid shelters.

In those days, the adult world revolved around the news. If they weren't huddled around the wireless listening to the BBC, they were anxiously scanning newspapers or discussing the day's event with friends and neighbors. There was no longer time for walks in the country or story telling around the fire or picnics in the hills. "Don't you know there's a war on?" everybody snapped at everybody else.

We couldn't take the train to London anymore to spend a day at the zoo or Madame Tussaud's because, "There's a war on, darlings. How many times must we tell you?" And, "No, of course we can't go to see a pantomime this year. Good heavens! It's far too dangerous."

We couldn't have new clothes, or new shoes or big fires or chocolate or fruit or hot water or a penny for a "sweetie" at the village shop because, "There's a war on…"

"Bloody old Hitler," Charles and I muttered to each other when every idea we ever had was squelched because, "There's a war on…"

"Will Father Christmas still be able to come?" we worried as December grew near. "What if the ack-ack gunners get him mixed up with the German bombers and shoot him down when he flies over England?"

"Don't worry," improvised our resourceful mother. "I'm sure he's thought of that and made arrangements with the gunners and the searchlight people. Some special code perhaps. Or maybe," she laughed, "Mrs. Christmas will have made him a special camouflage suit this year and he'll wear a helmet."

We didn't laugh with her. We wanted Father Christmas safe in his red suit and fur-trimmed hat and big black boots.

"How will he ever find our house?" Charles wondered out loud, "With all the blackout curtains closed and no lights showing anywhere, it'll be impossible."

"Don't be so silly," Mummy answered. "Of course

he'll find us. You both seem to have forgotten that he's magic. And so are his reindeers. Why, he can find the tiniest child in the darkest place. Now stop bothering me. You simply must remember there's a war on." She turned to me. "Here, hold up your hands. There's just time before tea to wind up one more ball of wool."

Reluctantly I did so, propping my elbows on the table, my hands held up stiffly. The skein of wool was slipped over them and we began the ritual I hated because it made my arms ache and my elbows sore.

Everybody knitted, of course. Even, it was said, the Queen and her two princesses in the palace. My own efforts were such a grubby mess of tangled wool and dropped stitches that I kept them hidden under a cushion in the sitting room as much as I could. But my mother was very skilled and turned out an astonishing number of socks, scarves, pullovers, cardigans and caps. She and her group from the Women's Institute knitted every scrap of wool they could get their hands on and when they could find none, ripped out outgrown, outworn clothing and, piecemeal, made what they could for "the boys" out there fighting in the bitter cold.

Most of Mummy's knitting was done in khaki but once in a while she would manage to get her hands on some navy blue wool and this she knitted with special care for it would go to David. David, her eldest son. Her pride and joy. Her personal ambassador to that hellish war. David who we all missed and worried about almost more than we could bear.

He was our senior by many years. Thirteen when Charles was born, fourteen when I came along. He was our hero. Big and brave. Strong and clever. He taught us everything. How to tie our shoes, how to climb trees, how to whistle, how to make the dog do tricks, how to tell time. David knew the names of birds and flowers and how to make us laugh when we wanted to cry.

Before the war, when he was still in school, our days seemed endless until it was time for him to come home. Then we sat out by our front gate, in every kind of weather, waiting for him to round the corner at the end of our road and when his bicycle came into view, it was a race to be the first to greet him, to be the one hoisted up onto the crossbar of the bike and pushed, smirking with pleasure, back up the hill to the house by big, wonderful David.

When he joined the Navy, sailors were all we could think about. We soon knew every ship in the fleet, every insignia, every rank. And further, when our parents tuned into the BBC for the six o'clock news, we joined them, avid for word of the sea battles, yet, at the same time, with hearts in our mouths that the news might be bad. When it was good, we swelled with pride as though it was not England or Mr. Churchill or the whole fleet but David, single-handed, who had sunk one more enemy destroyer, one more submarine, and gained us another victory.

Twice a day the Postman toiled up our hill, pushing his red bicycle with the royal insignia emblazoned on the crossbar. And twice a day our hopes were raised or dashed as he turned into our gate and laboriously shuffled through the cache of letters taken from the battered leather satchel slung across his shoulder.

"Looks like the good Lord spared 'im then, don't it?" he'd remark dolefully when his search produced a letter. Or, "'aven't 'eard for weeks now, 'ave you?" he'd commiserate, his long face growing longer as his hands came up empty. "Dirty business this 'ere war. I 'ad my way, I'd go over finish that 'itler off with me bare hands, so 'elp me, I would…"

At the end of October we went nearly mad with joy when, piecing together one of David's heavily censored letters, Mummy concluded he was due a forty-eight hour leave.

"When will he be here then?" we clambered breathlessly. But pore over the letter as she might, she could not wring that information from it.

"If he wrote the dates at all, they've cut them out," she said with disgust. "We'll just have to get his room ready and wait."

What a torment, after that letter, to leave home for school each day. What if he came home while we were gone? Only forty-eight hours and half of it to be spent travelling down from Scotland! Why, he'd only be home for a few hours!

"It can't be helped," Mummy said, firmly steering us out the door. "It might be days or even weeks before he gets here. Off you go. War or no war, you must go to school."

But it wasn't days or even weeks. October gave way to November, bleak and bitterly cold. And the war worsened. Scarcely a day passed that we weren't routed from home or school, or worse, our beds, to struggle into coats, grab the hated gas mask, and race pell-mell to the shelters while bombers droned overhead and searchlights lit up the skies.

The evening news became such an ordeal, the concern on the adults' faces so intense that, the minute tea was cleared away each day I took refuge under the dining room table. There, hidden by the heavy velvet cloth that covered it when not in use, and accompanied by my doll and sometimes the dog or cat, I remained until the radio was turned off and it was time for a bedtime story and a cup of watery cocoa.

It was around this time that the first of the "evacuees" started to straggle into our village from London.

First came the children. White faced, terrified, homeless. Not just orphans, though there were plenty of those, but others, too, whose parents, obliged to stay on in London themselves, still wanted their children out of the smoking nightmare the city had become.

Later came adults. People whose homes had been blown away and who were thrown on the mercy of total strangers for food and shelter. Anyone with a room to spare took them in. The first of these we came to know were a tired looking, elderly couple who came to stay with the widow Brown who lived next door. I remember going with my parents to greet them on a moonless night and all of us groping to find the handle of the front door in the blacked-out house.

Inside, the little front sitting room was packed with neighbors and villagers come in curiosity to hear and talk firsthand with these victims of the bombings.

"Bloody bomb landed smack on the roof," snorted the little Cockney man with a mirthless grin that showed missing teeth. "I said to the missus, I said, 'Blimey Gladys, me old girl, they've been and gone and done for us this time. Nothin' for it now but pack our bags and be on our way.' " His smile faded. "Wasn't thinkin' that we 'adn't no bags to pack… Nothin' to pack in 'em… Just what we 'ad on our backs… So 'ere we are, then. We'll do our best about the place. 'elp where we can till we gets on our feet. Must be some work hereabouts what with all the boys gone, In't that right, Gladys?"

From her seat by the meager fire Gladys nodded. "It's me boys I'm bothered about," she said, almost apologetically. "Now we ain't got no 'ome, how're they ever going to find us when this lot's over?" She brushed away a tear.

"Now then, Gladys, old girl," her husband warned. "Don't start! You 'eard the bloke in London same as me.

Said as 'ow they'd take care of all that. Said soon's this bloody 'itler's out the road we'll have no trouble findin' our boys, nor them us. In't that right?" He turned to our circle of listening faces.

"Absolutely…"

"No trouble at all…"

"Certainly you'll find your boys…" He was assured with more conviction than anyone could possibly have felt.

The head of the Home Guard of our village, stepped forward then and after clearing his throat a time or two, stammered out an awkward speech about how he and the others present had taken into account how difficult it must be for them to find themselves among strangers with no home and no job and no money. Thrusting an envelope towards the little Cockney he went on, "… and to that end we have taken up a small collection to see you through until such time as you may find employment…" He trailed off seeing the indignant color staining the man's cheeks, and hastily added, "By way of a loan, of course, old chap…"

Somewhat mollified, 'Arry, as he was called, reached out and reluctantly took the envelope. "So long as hits a loan, Guv'nor, s'alright then. Me an' the missus is much obliged." He glanced about the room taking in everyone present. "Ta ever so, I'm sure…"

There was an awkward little silence then that Mrs. Birch hurried to fill with her teapot. In the ensuing babble of voices I felt Charles tug at my cardigan sleeve.

"We could give them the money we've saved," he suggested in a whisper.

"No we can't." I gasped. "It's all we've got for David's Christmas present."

He shrugged. "They don't have anything to eat," he said, his eyes huge. "They don't have any anything…"

I stared at him without seeing him, my mind occupied with the pearl-handled penknife displayed in the window of the village shop with all its different little blades fanning out in every direction. "But David must have that knife," I insisted. "If the Germans ever caught him, he could use it to escape."

Charles shook his head stubbornly. "David won't let the Germans catch him," he said. "He's much too clever. Besides, how could they? He's on a ship. And we can always start saving up all over again." He stood up. "I'm going to get the money."

"No, don't go," I pleaded. "We only need another sixpence to get the knife. It'll take us ages and ages to save up that much again. Maybe even until next Christmas…"

But Charles wasn't listening and I turned away sulkily as he threaded his way through the grown-ups and left the room.

Anger stung my eyes when, minutes later, I saw him crossing the room with our penny jar held in both hands before him. Silently, he offered it to the tired old couple as the room about us quieted and all eyes fixed on the boy and his treasure.

"What's this, then?" Harry asked with a look that at the time I didn't understand but that I now realize showed that the last thing in the world he wanted was to accept anymore gifts from any more strangers, least of all the offerings of a child.

Harry was too old and too tired to play at a gratitude he didn't feel and didn't want. He'd had enough. More than likely his wish would have been to curse and shake his fist at the fates that had thrown him in a corner of someone else's home, the unwilling center of attention in a roomful of strangers.

And still Charles waited, not understanding the silence and with growing doubt as to the rightness of his actions that tied his tongue and caused his anxious eyes to shift from Harry and search the other waiting adult faces for a sign of approval. His arms holding out the money lost their authority and sagged a little, as though the small jar were too heavy for them.

I felt myself blushing though I didn't know why and then I heard my father clear his throat and I hoped with all my being that he would say something clever, or anything at all for that matter, that would break the awful, suffocating silence in the room.

But, "Take the money, 'Arry," Gladys said, quietly but firmly. "It in't charity. The boy just wants to give us a 'and till we gets settled, in't that right, luv?"

She left her seat by the fire and stood with her arm around Charles and so tiny was she that they stood shoulder to shoulder facing Harry who, with lowered head showing reddening neck, seemed ready to explode with the conflict of emotions going on inside him.

"It's my sister's too," Charles said earnestly. "We both saved it up."

"And where's your sister, then?" 'Arry asked on a great exhalation of breath, reaching out and taking the jar from Charles. "Blimey!" he went on with a wink, pretending the jar was too heavy for him. "You'll 'ave to 'elp me with this lot Gladys, me old girl. Must be a ruddy fortune in this 'ere jar. Looks like you'n me'll be living high off the hog for a long time with this lot, don't it?"

"It's ever such a lot, 'Arry," Gladys agreed solemnly, standing now beside her husband, the jar on the mantelpiece before them.

By then, blushing even more furiously than before, I had been pushed forward and stood beside Charles who was beaming at the couple.

"Me 'n 'Arry says, Ta ever so," Gladys said, fingering the skirt of her threadbare dress with red, workworn hands. "We're ever so glad of your 'elp…." Again she seemed about to collapse into tears which Harry stopped with a sharp jab of the elbow and a muttered, "Don't start, Gladys…"

"I think we could all use a drink." my father said

coming into the room carrying the decanter from the sideboard at home that contained, I knew, the last of the whisky that was being saved for David's return.

"Don't mind if I do, Guv'nor," Harry said, brightening.

"But that's David's whisky," I said indignantly.

"Never mind David," Daddy said firmly. "David's doing quite well for himself with a tot of rum every day on board ship. We're the chaps that need it."

"Hear, hear!" someone called amidst laughter.

"A toast!" came a voice from the back of the room when Mrs. Brown had found glasses for everyone.

"Long live England!"

"God save the King!"

"Down with the Huns!"

"Rule Britannia!"

And soon, despite the gravity of the situation, the house rang with laughter. My mother hustled Charles and me home soon after that but long into the night we could hear the singing next door. "It's a long way to Tipperary," "Hang Out Your Troubles on the Siegfried Line," "Lili Marlene," "Should Auld Acquaintance." And later still, the voices of Harry and Gladys singing "Knees Up Mother Brown" and other songs from the London music halls.

We loved having Harry and Gladys living next door and when Harry came home from his job as a bus conductor and Gladys from her's at the dairy, Charles and I spent as much time as we could with them although Mummy constantly threatened to stop these visits if we persisted in imitating their Cockney accents.

Within a week of their arrival they had returned the money jar to us and when our parents protested the extra sixpence we counted, Harry was adamant.

"Lord luv us, Guv'nor," he protested. "Hits hinterest. You takes a loan, you pays your hinterest and that's what me'n Gladys done. Paid hinterest. All proper like…"

And so we bought the beautiful pearl-handled knife for David and laid it very carefully on a scrap of red silk from the rag bag in an empty cigarette tin that Daddy gave us and wrapped the whole business in brown paper and string tied in a million knots and still… No David.

"He'll be here before the end of the month, you'll see," Mummy assured us as we sat before the fire cracking walnuts for the Christmas cake, always made a month early, one silver-frost night in November.

And again, "He's bound to be here any day now," she said in early December as she grated carrots as a substitute for the no longer available fruits she was accustomed to putting in her Christmas puddings. "Here," she said drying a handful of silver threepenny pieces and handing them to us to throw into the rich batter, "Make a wish."

"I know what you wished," Charles said to me.

"I wished the same as you," I said, sticking my tongue

out at him. "I wished that David would come home soon."

"You're not supposed to tell your wishes," Mummy reminded us, pouring the pudding mixture into basins. "But never mind. David will be home soon, never fear."

I doubted her. For the first time in my short life I doubted her and if the rest of the house hadn't been so cold, with the sitting room fire not to be lit until five o'clock, I would have left her and Charles and their silly, stupid ideas that David was coming home and gone away to sulk.

As it was, "I hate that stupid Mr. Hitler," I sobbed. "And I hate you!

"You're always saying that David is coming home when you know perfectly well he isn't. You tell lies!"

"Sarah!" Mummy and Charles gasped in unison.

"It's not true," I wailed, as shocked by my outburst as Charles and Mummy were. In shame, I flung myself at my mother and locked my arms around her waist. "I don't hate you, Mummy. I don't. I don't!"

"I know you don't, darling" she comforted. "And try not to worry. David will come home soon, you'll see. And we're not going to let that wicked old Hitler spoil Christmas for us either. Look, I bought these colored papers the other day in Woolworth's and I want you and Charles to make some chains for me."

She pulled open a drawer of the old kitchen dresser

and brought out a stack of brilliantly colored sheets of stiff paper. "Look, I'm going to make you a paste of flour and water and then you'll cut a strip of this red paper... Mind you cut it straight... Like this, see. And then you'll dab some paste on each end like this... And stick them together and pinch them tight for a minute so they hold...And then cut a strip of green and slip it through the red circle and stick that together. And soon you'll each have chains a mile long and we'll hang them in the hall and the sitting room and even in the dining room if we have enough. We'll leave them up until David comes home, even if it's after Christmas, and be blowed to old Mr. Hitler."

Soon the kitchen was knee-deep in paper chains and when Daddy came home, forgetting the cold of the house, we hung them in all the downstairs rooms and threaded them through the banisters.

"This weekend we'll go out and find some holly and evergreens," Daddy promised. "Maybe even some mistletoe, if we're lucky."

We filled two sacks full of brilliantly berrried holly and evergreens the next Sunday afternoon and Charles climbed a tree to cut down a clump of mistletoe. At home we poked it all behind every picture in the house and laid it along the mantelpieces of every room and added it to the chains on the stairway. And Christmas was only two days away and not a word from David.

"If he can't come, he can't come," Mummy said,

finally giving in to the inevitable on Christmas Eve. She said it matter of factly but her quick smile was missing and watching her I grew up a little, realizing for the first time that her need to have him home, to see for herself that he was well, was much, much greater than ours.

"Never mind," I said, relishing a suddenly discovered role of comforter. "You know he can't help it. You'll just have to manage with Charles and me, that's all."

"That's right," Charles agreed. "And since tomorrow is Christmas day, I'm going to get up first and bring you a nice hot cup of tea in bed the way David used to do."

"Darlings, darlings," Mummy laughed. "Of course I'll make do with you two and jolly lucky I am to have you! I used to wonder why you both arrived so long after David and now I know. It was so I could have you with me when he went away. And no thank you, Charles, darling, no tea in bed for me tomorrow. I shall have far too much to do stuffing that bird your father brought home. And don't forget we've got Mrs. Brown and Harry and Gladys coming here at one to help us eat it. The day after perhaps."

By teatime that day, Charles and I were shivery with excitement. Father Christmas, our Mother told us, had definitely left the North Pole and was even then hurtling towards England. With that news David, for once, was completely forgotten.

After tea was cleared away, the blackout curtains drawn against the damp, foggy night, the fire built up to pre-war stature and chestnuts set along the grate to roast, the house filled with friends and neighbors come to visit and sing carols and sip appreciatively of the whisky Daddy had mysteriously produced. But Charles and I wanted no part of it. We wanted to go to bed, pleaded to go to bed, the quicker to bring Christmas morning to us.

We didn't have the elaborate stockings of the sort that my children now hang, just one each of a pair of our father's everyday knee-length wool socks. But what a production he made of giving them to us! Inspecting and discarding half-a-dozen pairs from the top drawer of his dresser while we stood shivering in the icy hallway, waiting for him to find just the right pair. And then, the choice made, scurrying to our room and diving into bed to hug our hot water bottles and watch him tack them up to the mantelpiece over the unlit grate.

"How will we know when Father Christmas comes?" I whispered to Charles the minute I heard the sitting room door close downstairs on Daddy's back.

"I never know when he comes," Charles grumbled. "I stayed awake all night last Christmas Eve but I didn't catch him. There's a sure way to know he's been though."

"What?"

"After he's filled the stockings he doesn't hang them up again. They're too heavy. So he lays them across the bottom of the bed and if you push your feet down you can feel the weight. They weigh about a ton."

Experimentally, I eased my foot down the bed a little way but the sheets outside my little cocoon were like ice and I quickly pulled back.

"I'm staying awake to see him," I said firmly.

In the darkness I heard Charles snort. "You can't," he scoffed. "You're still a baby. But this year, I expect I will. And as soon as he gets here, I'll wake you."

"Promise?"

"Promise."

Pale light was seeping through a tiny chink in the tightly drawn blackout curtains when I awakened the next morning and, of course, I didn't remember what day it was, but as I stretched, my foot passed beneath an unaccustomed weight.

"Charles!" I screeched, my breath puffing white before me. "Wake up. It's Christmas!"

Forgetting the bitter cold, I dived across the room to turn on the lights and was back sitting up in bed before Charles was fully awake. Slowly I drew the long, gray sock towards me, marveling at the wonderful lumpiness of it and the delicious crackling sounds coming from within.

There have been dozens of Christmases in my life since that one. Christmases that brought to me and my family more beautifully wrapped gifts than an entire living room in a well heated house could contain, yet there has never been one that matched that one for the wonder and excitement I felt as, with hands numb with cold, I wonderingly felt the strange lumps and hollows of that old gray sock and groped inside to pull out one little treasure after another.

A miniature tea set, each little piece wrapped separately in a crumbly wisp of tissue paper. A gold mesh bag full of chocolate coins, each one covered in heavy gold foil and embossed to look like a real coin. A tissue-wrapped match box which, when I slid open its drawer, revealed a string of bright, shiny beads. Another containing a tiny pin shaped like the Queen's crown, wonderfully set with dazzling glass that shimmered in the light. A little whistle. And nuts and apples and oranges and toffees until the folds of my eiderdown were filled with wonder and I daren't move my legs for fear of sending my wonderful treasures crashing to the floor.

From Charles' bed I heard little exclamations of delight. "A soldier! A knight! A sailor… just like David! A car! What a beauty! A whistle!" But I didn't look. I was too happily absorbed with my own.

And when the last wonder had been removed and the socks were limp and out of shape, "Look!" Charles exclaimed, pointing to the chest of drawers against the wall opposite our beds and there, lined up to the foot of mine, sat the most beautiful doll I had ever seen. She smiled at me with red lips and through her real curling eyelashes her brilliant blue eyes sparkled. Golden curls sprouted from beneath her green velvet, feather bedecked bonnet and she wore little black, patent leather shoes on her white-stockinged feet. Around her neck a wisp of fur decorated her green velvet coat. I was to learn, years later, that my mother had finished making that splendid costume only minutes before we wakened. But that morning I saw her as a very special gift from Father Christmas and I slid out of bed as though it were greased, nuts and apples and oranges thudding to the floor as I reached for her and bumped into Charles as he groped for the brightly painted engine and two cars that were on his side of the dresser.

And then we were each back under the covers, examining the wonder of the splendid gifts that Father Christmas had magically brought to us.

"Happy Christmas!" sang Mummy's voice from downstairs and we heard the familiar sound of her footsteps coming upstairs and the chink of teaspoons rattling in saucers and knew it was a special day indeed if we were to have tea in bed.

The door opened slowly, the way a door does when the person opening it is balancing a tray. Hurriedly I sat up in bed, my doll in my arms, watching it and then my breath stopped short, and for a moment, just a tiny second, the words on my lips died as I stared in wonder at what blazed that Christmas into my memory forever.

Above my Mother's laughing face, set at a jaunty angle, was David's uniform cap and grinning at us over her shoulder, David himself!

Sheelagh Mawe was born in Hertfordshire, England. She subsequently lived in France where she worked first as a tour guide for Champagne Mercier in Epernay and then as a bi-lingual secretary for the American Express Company in Paris. Moving to Florida some years later with her three children, she became a tennis enthusiast and worked as General Manager of a tennis club. She now lives in Orlando, Florida.

TOTALLY UNIQUE THOUGHTS
... because thoughts become things.

Launched in 1989 by two brothers and their cool mom, TUT believes that everyone's special, that every life is meaningful, and that we're all here to learn that dreams really do come true.

We also believe that "thoughts become things," and that imagination is the gift that can bring love, health, abundance and happiness into our lives.

Totally Unique Thoughts
TUT Enterprises, Inc.
Orlando, Florida
www.tut.com
USA